THE HAMLYN LECTURES
TWENTY-SECOND SERIES

THE ENGLISH JUDGE

AUSTRALIA
The Law Book Company Ltd.
Sydney : Melbourne : Brisbane

CANADA AND U.S.A.
The Carswell Company Ltd.
Agincourt, Ontario

INDIA
N. M. Tripathi Private Ltd.
Bombay

ISRAEL
Steimatzky's Agency Ltd.
Jerusalem : Tel Aviv : Haifa

MALAYSIA : SINGAPORE : BRUNEI
Malayan Law Journal (Pte) Ltd.
Singapore

NEW ZEALAND
Sweet & Maxwell (N.Z.) Ltd.
Wellington

PAKISTAN
Pakistan Law House
Karachi

THE
ENGLISH JUDGE

BY

HENRY CECIL

*His Honour H. C. Leon, M.C., M.A., LL.B., formerly
one of Her Majesty's Judges of County Courts*

Published under the auspices of
THE HAMLYN TRUST

LONDON
STEVENS & SONS
1970

Published in 1970 by
Stevens & Sons Limited of
11 New Fetter Lane in the
City of London and printed
in Great Britain by The
Eastern Press Ltd. of London
and Reading

SBN 420 43350 3

CONTENTS

(George Orwell's " hanging judge "—integrity of judges long established—" summing up for a conviction "—solicitors' eligibility
as judges—the Lord Chancellor's unique position considered—
how other judges are appointed—county court registrars—
background of today's judges—marriage and outside interests—
educational trend of last forty years—final Bar Examination
results—contact between judges and students—public image
of today's judges—some criminals' views—some other opinions,
including a schoolboy's.)

(More opinions about judges—the Communist view—the status
of irremovability—judicial abuse of power—solicitors occasionally criticised unfairly—jokes in court—private interviews
between judge and counsel—a scandalous case—should judges
have a trial run before appointment?—a sabbatical year on
appointment?—the judges' rules—effect of a case upon third
parties.)

(Another schoolboy's comments considered at length—" judicial
ignorance "—contempt of court—the *Welsh* case—some judges'
lack of imagination—why does a witness have to be old, ill or
pregnant to get a seat?—why 2,000 people went to prison each
year by mistake—putting witnesses at ease—the oath—remoteness of some judges—judges' private lives—problem of the
motor car—judges' holidays—judges' care to avoid appearance
of favouritism—trial of accident cases—national insurance
instead?—injustice due to lack of imagination.)

THE HAMLYN LECTURES

THE HAMLYN TRUST

THE Hamlyn Trust came into existence under the will of the late Miss Emma Warburton Hamlyn, of Torquay, who died in 1941, at the age of eighty. She came of an old and well-known Devon family. Her father, William Bussell Hamlyn, practised in Torquay as a solicitor for many years. She was a woman of strong character, intelligent and cultured, well versed in literature, music and art, and a lover of her country. She inherited a taste for law, and studied the subject. She also travelled frequently on the Continent and about the Mediterranean, and gathered impressions of comparative jurisprudence and ethnology.

Miss Hamlyn bequeathed the residue of her estate in terms which were thought vague. The matter was taken to the Chancery Division of the High Court, which on November 29, 1948, approved a Scheme for the administration of the Trust. Paragraph 3 of the Scheme is as follows:—

" The object of the charity is the furtherance by lectures or otherwise among the Common People of the United Kingdom of Great Britain and Northern Ireland of the knowledge of the Comparative Jurisprudence and the Ethnology of the chief European countries including the United Kingdom, and the circumstances of the growth of such jurisprudence to the intent that the Common People of the United Kingdom may realise the privileges which in law and custom they enjoy in comparison with other European Peoples and realising and appreciating such privileges may recognise the responsibilities and obligations attaching to them."

From the first the Trustees decided to organise courses of lectures of outstanding interest and quality by persons of eminence, under the auspices of co-operating universities or other bodies, with a view to the lectures being made available in book form to a wide public.

The Twenty-second Series of Hamlyn Lectures was delivered in December, 1970, by Henry Cecil in Gray's Inn.

J. N. D. ANDERSON,

December, 1970.   *Chairman of the Trustees.*

NOTE OF THANKS

I WISH to record my gratitude to Mrs. Portia Holland and Miss Lindsay Megarry for the very great assistance which they have given me in the research necessary to enable me to deliver these lectures. Their help was invaluable.

I also wish to thank very much indeed my old friend Frank Gahan, Q.C., who took immense trouble over reading the manuscript of these lectures and made many helpful suggestions, most of which I have adopted.

Finally, I am most grateful to the Treasurer and Masters of the Bench of Gray's Inn for their kindness in making arrangements for the lectures to be delivered in Gray's Inn Hall.

HENRY CECIL

CHAPTER 1

BACKGROUND OF THE JUDGES [1]

In February 1941 George Orwell in his essay *England Your England* wrote this:

> "*The hanging judge—that evil old man in scarlet robe and horsehair wig, whom nothing short of dynamite will ever teach what century he is living in, but who will at any rate interpret the law according to the books and will in no circumstances take a money bribe—is one of the symbolic figures of England.*"

These lectures are partly concerned with the judges whom Orwell so described and with their contemporary brethren, but my main concern is with their present-day successors in England and Wales. (I hope that Welshmen will forgive my subsequent use of England as including Wales for the sake of brevity.)

But before I embark on the subject-matter of the lectures, I must say how deeply I appreciate the altogether surprising honour which the trustees of the Hamlyn Trust have done me in asking me to deliver them, for I am well aware that I cannot approach in erudition or knowledge any of my illustrious predecessors.

[1] As a glance at the summaries will show, the heading to each lecture is intended as a label rather than a comprehensive title.

A number of books have been written, papers published and lectures delivered on the judicial function. Outstanding examples are those of Lord Diplock, Mr. Justice Lawton and Mr. Justice MacKenna. There would not be much point in my attempting to do the same thing. My effort would simply fail by comparison and add nothing.

Accordingly what I shall be attempting to do is to present, as objectively as a former county court judge can, a picture of the modern judge publicly and (to a lesser extent) privately, with all his virtues and imperfections, both as he appears to me and as he appears to the public. By " judge " I mean all those whose main work is the trial of cases or appeals, and this, of course, includes stipendiary magistrates and justices of the peace. Although I shall refer to them shortly, I am not including in my survey recorders and chairmen or deputy-chairmen of quarter sessions, except for the full-time recorders and full-time chairmen and deputy-chairmen. Many deputy-chairmen are county court judges. The remainder of the recorders and chairmen and deputy-chairmen only sit as judges a few times a year.

I have investigated the known background of close on half the full-time professional judges and shall state where they were educated, how many of them marry, how they fared in their final Bar Examinations, what their hobbies are and so on.

I have also made extensive inquiries from most sections of the population (in and out of prison) to find out what people, who are able to express an opinion, think of the present judges. I should like to thank very much indeed all those who have given me their views on the subject. They have been of immense help to me and I can assure the writers that the fact that by reason of lack of time and space I am only able to give actual quotations from a very small percentage of them does not mean that I have not used them. On the contrary they have been of the greatest possible use to me in preparing these lectures.

I shall make certain suggestions for improvements in the method of appointing judges and in the way in which they administer justice. I was a judge for eighteen years and, therefore, at any rate had the chance of seeing where the wheels of justice seemed to creak. Moreover I was probably guilty of most of the faults which give rise to my suggestions for improvements. So could a convicted safe-breaker give valuable advice to his unlawful successor in the business.

I must say at the outset that I am unable to comply with that part of the object of the Hamlyn Trust which provides that the lectures are intended to help the common people of the United Kingdom to realise the privileges which in law and custom they enjoy *in comparison with other European peoples.* (The italics are mine.) Although I could have obtained second-hand knowledge of judges in other European countries, I do not think that anyone who has not worked for some years at least under the system obtaining in those countries can fairly compare any part of their systems with our own.

Many people will know that in other European countries judges are in fact appointed quite differently from the way in which they are appointed here. In England, High Court and county court judges are appointed entirely from the Bar but elsewhere in Europe there is a separate judicial profession. When you start your career in the law there, you have to make up your mind whether you wish to go on the judicial or the advocates' side. In those countries there are thousands of full-time professional judges; in England, under 300.

The difference is mainly due to our use of justices. They

do over 98 per cent. of the criminal work in the country and quite an amount of civil work as well. While I may think that our system is the better, I have no personal experience to justify my saying that it is. So I hope that the shade of Miss Hamlyn will be satisfied if I show that our system is a good one and make suggestions for improving it. I am relieved to find that some at least of my predecessors have apparently taken the same view and have not attempted to compare the two systems.

These lectures are normally attended mainly by lawyers and I must therefore apologise to the lawyers among you for stating things which are already very well known to you but I must do this because by the terms of the Hamlyn Trust the lectures are to be delivered to the common people of the United Kingdom. The vast majority of the people are not lawyers and I want, if possible, to include in these lectures most of the facts which an ordinary member of the public might want to know about the modern judge. I shall put some of them in an appendix to this first lecture to avoid cluttering it up with too many facts and figures.

First I propose to deal with Orwell's " evil old man." I do not believe for a moment that, in saying that the judge would not take " a money bribe," Orwell meant to imply that he would take a couple of pheasants or be otherwise corrupt in any way. The reputation for integrity on the English Bench has been established so firmly and for so long that even the denigrators of English judges do not suggest that they do not still bear and justly bear that reputation.

What then did Orwell mean by " evil old man "? I was called to the Bar in 1923 and, by the time Orwell wrote his essay, I had appeared a good deal in front of all the judges who could have been included in his assertion. None of them was an evil old man in the ordinary sense of those words. The average age of the eighteen King's Bench judges (the only judges who normally tried criminal cases) was just under 61. The oldest was 73 and the youngest 50, eight were under 60 and only three were 70 or over. The average age of all thirty-five Court of Appeal and High Court judges was just over 61. The oldest was 73 and the youngest 45. Their average age on appointment was 53.

What did Orwell mean by " evil "? It cannot have been because on a conviction for murder the judge passed sentence of death, as Orwell must have known that a judge had no option as far as the penalty was concerned. Possibly he believed that some judges enjoyed passing the death sentence. I do not doubt that the majority of them thought that we should have a death penalty and I do not doubt that some of them thought that the persons accused in front of them ought to be convicted and that it was desirable in the interests of the public that they should be executed, but, looking at the list of names I have in front of me, I can say without qualification that it is utterly ludicrous to suggest that any of them enjoyed passing the death sentence. I have seen all of them in action. How many of them had Orwell seen? He certainly had no evidence upon which he could describe any of them as " evil " in the sense that he enjoyed sending a man to the gallows.

What Orwell more probably had in mind were murder cases where, in his opinion, the judge unfairly " secured " a conviction, with the result that the accused was hanged. Although we no longer have a death penalty, complaints are still made that judges on occasion sum up unfairly and I have received a number of allegations of bias.

A student visited the assizes and was favourably impressed by the judge. Nevertheless he said:

" On the whole I think he was as fair as is humanly possible, but in one of the cases I saw I fear that the judge was slightly biassed in favour of the prosecution." (For the remainder of his comments see pages 36–37.)

This young man was obviously not prejudiced against judges but he thought he detected bias. It is of course perfectly possible that in the case to which he referred, the evidence for the prosecution was overwhelming, and in such a case it may be difficult for a judge to sum up without appearing to lean towards the prosecution. The mere recitation of the evidence might give an appearance of bias. But this complaint of bias comes too often for it to be explained away in every case. Here is a much stronger criticism, also from a student:

" The image of the English judge as portrayed by television splits fairly easily into two groups, one the fat and fairly bumbling fool who is getting everything wrong. Until recently I had no reason to believe that this was untrue, although one does not take these things quite literally and it is obvious that judges are men of integrity rather than of senility. The other portrayal is the quiet man more or less in the background, sustaining the odd objection. This is perhaps nearer to my ideas. As a result of these preconceived ideas it was quite a shock to me to discover, at the assizes anyway, how very active the judge was and how he made every little detail plain to the jury. The main thing about the proceedings that shocked me were the cutting remarks and many quips that the judge made with impunity almost. This shattered my ideas completely and I felt sometimes during the proceedings that he was definitely biassed. It seemed at times plain that he was confident of the defendant's guilt and, although he made up for this by stressing to the jury that it was on the facts stated they must go and that they must be quite sure of the prisoner's guilt, it didn't do much to remedy the harm he had done."

One of our oldest retired High Court judges used to make an amusing after-dinner speech in which he showed how it was possible for a judge summing up to say things which sounded admirably fair in print—in case the matter went to appeal—but which by reason of emphasis or tone of voice or the look on his face were calculated to have the opposite effect on the jury. Unfortunately, though exaggerated, there was a basis of truth in this brilliant performance.

I have received other complaints about judges' remarks during a trial, but I will deal with the " cutting remarks and quips " later under the heading of abuse of power. I want to continue now with the complaint of bias. I feel sure that this is the gist of Orwell's grievance. It is certainly the complaint of a student from a technical college, who writes:

" Up until recently the image of the typical English judge which I had was one of a very understanding and patient old fellow whose words were final and taken as gospel truth. I arrived at this conclusion from the impression I received from books, the theatre and television crime programmes. I was under the impression that he had no bearing upon a case whatsoever and that his only function was to keep the court in order and stop the whole thing from becoming a farce. But this opinion was completely shattered after a visit to the local assizes. I found the judge far from unbiased. In the case which I saw, the judge seemed to be on the side of the prosecution. This to me seems totally wrong. I believe that if more judges were like the mythical TV judges, then justice would be much fairer."

People of all ages have complained about some judges' apparent bias and every lawyer knows of cases where a judge " sums up for a conviction." I sympathise with judges who from their vast experience are satisfied not only that a particular man is guilty but that, if he is acquitted, he is likely to do the same thing again and that the public needs to be protected from such a man. Which is the greater harm? That an acquitted criminal should do it again or that judges should not appear to be fair-minded? Although a case can be made out for judges protecting the public at the expense of the appearance of justice, I personally have no doubt that in the long run the public would suffer more from judges acting unfairly than from wrongdoers being given an immediate opportunity to pursue their wrongdoing.

But the matter is not at all a simple one. The judge is not only sitting to see that the prisoner has a fair trial. The public is also entitled to a fair trial. As that great judge, Sir Matthew Hale, said some three hundred years ago: " When dealing with grave crimes, one must have pity on the country as well as on the prisoner." It is too easy to sympathise with the man in the dock because he is the person who stands in immediate jeopardy and to forget his unfortunate victim and, what may be almost as important or more important, further potential victims if the man is acquitted. The judge may have in front of him a man charged with the rape of a child, he may know that this man has been convicted of such a charge before and he may feel sure that, if the man is let loose, some other child, possibly many children, will suffer in a similar way. The only real evidence against the man may be that of the child, who suffered so terribly that she is really incapable of giving evidence properly. It would be wrong of such a judge, if he conducted the trial unfairly in order to secure the conviction of the man but, if he did so, could he properly be called " evil "?

There are certainly a few judges today who, in my view, seek to steer some cases unfairly towards a conviction. When I say " unfairly," I must make it plain that I am perfectly certain that this never happens when the judge has any doubt about the guilt of the accused. He feels sure of it, and in his desire to protect the public and, in some cases perhaps, in his desire that retribution should follow a particularly unpleasant crime, he bolsters up the case for the prosecution and denigrates that for the defence. It can be argued (I think wrongly) that the public is entitled to have such judges and that a little bias in favour of the public is no bad thing. After all, the public is paying the judge and the whole judicial system is for the benefit of the public. Why should the murderer or rapist get off just because the evidence is a little lacking in strength? Everybody " knows " he did it.

Personally I think that the possibility of an innocent man being convicted is so horrible that every care should be taken to avoid that possibility. It is for this reason that it is English law that a man cannot be convicted unless his guilt is proved beyond all reasonable doubt, and I do not believe that a judge's influence should be employed to overcome what may be a reasonable doubt in a jury's mind. But which is the more important? That the man with possibly several previous convictions for offences of violence should be acquitted because the evidence is too weak, or that another child should be saved from being grievously injured? Can a judge be blamed if he stretches a point in favour of the child? I would blame him, as would, I think, any lawyer, but I am not at all sure that he would be blamed by everyone in the Court of World Opinion.

For example, in the rape case to which I have referred, what man outside the legal profession, knowing the man's record, would not want to see the prisoner convicted? If only to protect other children. A judge has feelings like anyone else. Can he *think* (as opposed to behave) any differently from the layman? Owing to his training he is, or should be, capable of conducting the case with complete fairness towards the prisoner, with the probable result that he will be acquitted. Has such a judge acted with complete fairness towards the public or towards the little children who may be hurt in the future? One hears of the relatives or friends of a convicted man complaining at the unfairness of the summing-up of the judge, but what about the relatives or friends of an acquitted man's next victim? How many letters of abuse does a judge get from them? None. They are probably not aware of his existence. But, when the acquitted rapist strikes again, what are the thoughts of the judge who " summed up for an acquittal " if he reads about it? He would comfort himself with the thought that he had no alternative.

When people talk of justice, their opinion depends upon their point of view. " Oh, I know I was exceeding the speed limit, but it's only the policeman's word against mine and it isn't justice to take his word. How do they know I'm not telling the truth? "

On the other hand, when a man is charged with a horrible crime, the public would stretch a good many points to see him convicted. " Why be too technical? " they say. " If the law lets a man like that off, there must be something wrong with the law. It was a dreadful thing to do."

It is a valid criticism of a judge that he " sums up for a conviction." He should not, but, in some cases, would he be so blameworthy?

He is certainly not " evil " and there is but a small minority of judges who behave like this. But the complaints which I have received show that there are too many. It cannot be the case that complainants who come from different localities have by coincidence all happened to see the same judge or even the same two or three judges.

I have now dealt with one of the complaints against judges —bias. There are other complaints and most of them can be included under one of the following headings: abuse of power, remoteness and lack of imagination. I shall be dealing in detail with these matters later. Before I come to them, however, I want to describe the present full-time professional judges and it is only fair to point out that none of the criticisms to which I have referred, or will refer, applies to the great majority of them.

Their average age today is 60; their average age on appointment, 53. The youngest was appointed when he was 46. In the last forty years judges have been appointed younger than before but it will have been noticed that the average age of today's judges on appointment is the same as it was in 1941, 53. The youngest High Court judges to be appointed since 1935 were Lord Devlin (43) and Lord Hodson (42).

No judge appointed since December 17, 1959, may sit beyond the age of 75. Curiously enough, county court judges have to retire at the age of 72 but they can be given leave to sit until the age of 75. When they are given such leave, it is usually doled out year by year. The average county court judge has a lower standard of legal knowledge and intellectual capacity than the average High Court judge, but I cannot believe that such intellectual powers as he has diminish any faster than those of his superior brethren in the High Court. Perhaps some day someone will explain why it is necessary to keep an eye on the county court judge between the ages of 72 and 75 while the High Court judge can be left to his own devices. The same interpreter may also be able to explain why the retiring age for magistrates and justices is now 70.

Another curious distinction between High Court and county court judges is that, while both are appointed by the Sovereign, only the Sovereign at the request of both Houses of Parliament can remove a High Court judge, whereas the Lord Chancellor can remove a county court judge without a word to the Sovereign, though only for " inability or misbehaviour." This anomaly is probably because it is only since 1959 that county court judges have been appointed by the Sovereign on the recommendation of the Lord Chancellor. Up till then they had been appointed by the Lord Chancellor on his own. When the change was made in 1959 the provisions for removal may have been overlooked.

No judge, either High Court or county court, has ever been removed since 1700. Parliament has more than once made it clear that it will only ask for the removal of a judge if he has been guilty of some moral delinquency or has become hopelessly ill, *e.g.* insane. Merely being a bad judge or inter- rupting too often is not enough. Although Parliament could depart from this tradition if it wanted to, it has not done so for 270 years and it is very doubtful if it would. However, as I point out later, the influence of the Press and of the legal profession itself should be sufficient to secure the resignation of a really unsatisfactory judge.

I have received a number of complaints that High Court and county court judges are selected exclusively from the Bar. One law student says that this practice is indefensible. This is an important matter and requires consideration. The average solicitor is a person of complete integrity. There are many good lawyers among solicitors and the intellectual capacity of some of them is quite as high as that of some High Court judges. Why then should High Court and county court judges not be appointed from the ranks of solicitors? In my opinion there is one overriding reason.

There are about 2,400 practising members of the Bar. There are over 20,000 solicitors. Of the 2,400 practising members of the Bar some are too old, some are too young, some have not sufficient qualifications to justify elevation to the Bench. In the result, there are at any one time about 200–300 barristers—perhaps a few more—possibly not as many—who might be considered for appointment to the High Court or county court Bench. In order to be so considered, they would have practised for a good many years and will have become known to their colleagues and to many of the High Court judges. It is thus virtually impossible for anyone whose standard of integrity is not high enough for promotion to the Bench to receive such promotion. The Lord Chancellor and members of his department and the judges would nearly all know a good deal about every member of the Bar whose practice is big enough to justify his being considered for appointment to the Bench. In other words, no one who might conceivably spoil the tradition of integrity has any chance of getting through the sieving process.

There is no different standard of integrity between that of the barrister and that of the average solicitor but there are nearly ten times as many solicitors, they have greater temptations and do occasionally succumb to them. A very few of them go to prison. Four to five thousand complaints are made against them each year. No doubt the vast majority of these complaints have no foundation and of those which have foundation I imagine that the great majority are simply for lack of care, not for dishonesty. This can be inferred from the number of solicitors who are struck off or suspended. It averages only twelve struck off and six suspended per year.

There are only about fifty complaints made against barristers per year on an average, that is to say one in forty-eight as compared with one in five in the case of solicitors. But there is little difference between the comparative number of barristers disbarred and the comparative number of solicitors struck off or suspended. The average in the case of barristers is one and a half per year out of 2,400. This is not very different from the eighteen solicitors struck off or suspended out of 20,000. The difference in the number of complaints is no doubt due to the fact that solicitors deal directly with the public and barristers do not.

It can be seen, then, that the argument for rigidly maintaining the present qualification for appointment to the Bench is not based on different standards of integrity in the two professions, but on the vital necessity for the sieving process before a judge is appointed and on the existence of such a large number of solicitors.

If solicitors were equally available for appointment to the Bench and the professions were not fused, they would escape the sieving process altogether. They would never have acted as advocates before the High Court Bench and no High Court judge would have seen them in action in that capacity. Who could be sure that someone unsuitable might not slip through? The standard of honesty required of a barrister is the highest attainable. There are some who fall below that standard, but they do not become judges. It becomes known to their colleagues and to the Bench that they are not to be trusted in the full sense in which judges and barristers trust one another. Until a man practises as an advocate no one can be sure of his standard of integrity under stress. I have met solicitors who are completely honest in the ordinary sense of that word and who would no more think of converting their clients' moneys than of going out on a housebreaking expedition, but nevertheless they have not appreciated the extent of the integrity required of the barrister. This is no doubt partly due to the fact that they have not been brought up in their professional life in the tradition of the Bench and the Bar. The idea of slightly misleading a judge, let alone positively deceiving him, is anathema to the average barrister. The great majority of solicitors, both in the best-known and in the least-known firms, have an equally high standard of integrity. But there are undoubtedly a number in both categories who have not, just as there are barristers who do not come up to standard.

If the professions were fused, would the higher standard or the lower standard prevail among the new profession of 22,400 lawyers? Assuming that the higher standard prevailed, there would be 22,400 instead of 2,400 possible candidates for promotion to the Bench. However many of these could be eliminated on various grounds, there would still be far more than the comparatively few candidates available today. In consequence, some of them would be nothing like so well known to their fellow advocates or to the High Court Bench as the present limited number of starters, whose form has been fully exposed. It may be argued that, in view of the high standard of integrity among solicitors, the proportion of suitable candidates for appointment to the Bench would be the same as at present, but this is not the point, which is that it would be impossible for the far larger number of candidates to become properly known to High Court judges. And only those who practised as advocates would be known at all, or at all well.

There would be advantages to the public in fusion as well as other disadvantages, but, however great the advantages on balance, they could not outweigh the danger that the judicial reputation for integrity might be lost or diminished. It is one of our most important remaining assets and one of the few which the United States of America must envy. Nothing should be done which might conceivably involve a risk of its being lost.

The present position is not entirely unfair to solicitors. A solicitor who wishes to become a judge can be called to the Bar without taking certain examinations. To what extent he should have to eat his dinners is a matter for consideration. Although not many solicitors do become barristers, the percentage of those making the change who are subsequently elevated to the Bench is very high.

Today a barrister can start to earn quite a substantial amount within a very short time of finishing his pupillage, so that a solicitor who became a barrister need not suffer a large diminution in his earnings, as he might have done some years ago.

Solicitors may be appointed stipendiary magistrates, and chairmen or deputy-chairmen of quarter sessions, but no magistrate has ever been appointed to a county court or High Court judgeship, since solicitors became eligible to be appointed magistrates. There is one solicitor chairman and a few solicitors are deputy-chairmen. Personally I think it is a pity that every candidate for a magistracy does not have to go through the sieving process, though I have no doubt that the one or two solicitors now on the Bench are of the highest integrity. The danger is that sometime someone unsuitable may slip through and we cannot afford one appointment of that kind.

The Beeching Commission, which recommended by a majority that solicitors should be eligible for appointment as circuit judges (the proposed new judges to replace county court judges), did not even refer to the vital consideration of integrity in expressing their opinion. It is to be hoped that Parliament will consider it most carefully before implementing this recommendation.

I set out in an Appendix to this lecture the order of precedence of the judges (as far as it is known), the qualifications for their appointment, their salaries, their pensions, the robes they wear and the cost of them. The salaries range from £14,500 for the Lord Chancellor to £5,300 for the lowest-paid stipendiary magistrate. But I must point out that owing to the increase in the cost of living these salaries are going up at intervals and that the figures given in the Appendix may not be up to date on the day on which they appear.

The House of Lords is the supreme court of appeal and, although theoretically all members of the House can sit to hear an appeal, by long-established practice only the Law Lords (the specially appointed life peers known as Lords of Appeal in Ordinary, and other peers who have held high judicial office) may vote on such appeals. When two lay peers sought to vote just under a hundred years ago their votes were ignored, a typically English procedure, and no one has tried it on since. But one day someone may and, if a majority of lay peers really insisted on trying to vote upon legal appeals, the law would have to be altered so as to exclude them.

None of the comments which I have received has criticised adversely the judges of the House of Lords. It is common experience at the Bar that, provided an advocate knows his facts and his law, it is the easiest court to address. Very rarely does the House consist of less than five judges and accordingly each judge has four colleagues to observe his behaviour. But, whether this has anything to do with it or not, the judicial mistakes in behaviour which are found in other courts are never found there, as far as my knowledge and experience go, and this is confirmed by my researches into public opinion.

The Supreme Court of Judicature, which includes the Court of Appeal and the High Court, is not supreme. When it was created it was intended at first by Parliament that it should be and that there should be no appeal to the House of Lords. During the discussion in Parliament, however, eventually the House of Lords was left as the supreme court of appeal but the name of what remained the lower court was not changed.

At the time of preparing these lectures (July 1970) the number of judges was under the permitted maximum, but, though the maximum is laid down by statute, it can be altered by Order in Council. Accordingly, the actual number is of more interest than the maximum. For the purpose of making my survey of the present judges, I took those sitting in July 1969. There were then, at that time, twenty-four Law Lords, eleven Lords Justices of Appeal, sixty-two High Court judges, ninety county court judges and forty-eight stipendiary magistrates. They totalled 235. There are a few more now. In addition to these judges, there are the Recorder of London, the Common Serjeant and the ten additional judges of the Central Criminal Court and the judge of the Mayor's and City of London Court. There are also the full-time Recorders of Liverpool and Manchester and four ancient judgeships in Durham, Lancaster, Liverpool and Salford. Then there are three Official Referees and also nineteen full-time chairmen or deputy-chairmen of quarter sessions.

I have investigated the background of 117 judges taken at random out of the 235 judges mentioned above. Although this number is under half the total of professional full-time judges, I do not imagine that it will be suggested that an investigation of the remainder of all the full-time professional judges would disclose any substantially different results from what I have found.

By the time I deliver these lectures the Beeching Report may or may not have been put into operation, wholly or partially. Ordinary recorders are likely to be abolished, forty new county court judges (who will all be called circuit judges) may be appointed, and 120 part-time judges (to be called recorders). It will not be a simple matter to appoint forty new judges of proved integrity and ability, all of whom will know how to behave on the Bench. It will certainly have to be done, as the Beeching Commission realises, by slow stages. The 120 recorders could be of some value as a nucleus from which to choose High Court and circuit judges, provided they sit for long enough and are under proper observation. In my next lecture I deal in detail with the desirability of prospective judges having a trial run.

There was a time—not so long ago—when politics played some part in the appointment of High Court judges, and a number of judgeships were given to barristers as a reward for political services. The results were not satisfactory. Fortunately since the 1939–45 war the practice has ceased and it is very important that it should not be restarted. It is to be hoped that the new practice (at present only twenty-five years old) will become as traditional as judges' integrity.

The Lord Chancellor is the only political appointment, but he is avowedly so. He is a member of the Government and is appointed by the Sovereign on the recommendation of the

Prime Minister. He stands or falls with the Government or can be asked to resign by the Prime Minister like any other Minister of the Crown. Curiously enough, while all other professional judges require substantial legal qualifications for their appointment, the Lord Chancellor requires none. No Prime Minister would today think of recommending a layman for appointment as Lord Chancellor but legally he could do so. There is a doubt (not yet resolved) as to whether a Roman Catholic can be appointed but otherwise there are no restrictions on the appointment.

It has been suggested by lawyers and others that the combination of judicial and political functions within the office of Lord Chancellor is not satisfactory. On the face of it, this appears to be a valid criticism. The idea of a High Court judge introducing a political measure in the House of Commons is today unthinkable. Yet the Lord Chancellor may do this very thing in the House of Lords. In theory, therefore, it seems difficult to argue in favour of the present position of the Lord Chancellor. In practice, however, it has worked extremely well, and no Lord Chancellor within living memory— or indeed well beyond living memory—has ever appeared to confuse his political with his judicial functions.

If it is asked how such a position could have arisen when it has long been traditional that judges should take no part in political matters, the answer is simply that this was not always traditional, and that there was a time very long ago when judges could in fact be Members of Parliament. But, though for a short time in 1806, Lord Ellenborough, the Chief Justice, was a member of the Cabinet, he was very hesitant about accepting the position and the tradition has by now been long established that, with the notable exception of the Lord Chancellor, judges should take no part whatever in politics. This one exception is inconsistent with the tradition, but, as it has been found to work perfectly well in practice, and as the Lord Chancellor is a very useful member of the Government, it would seem pointless to alter the position.

The Lord Chief Justice, Lords of Appeal in Ordinary, the Master of the Rolls (so called because of his original responsibility for the keeping of legal records), the President of the Probate,[2] Divorce and Admiralty Division and the Lords Justices of Appeal are appointed by the Sovereign on the recommendation of the Prime Minister. All other professional judges are appointed by the Sovereign on the recommendation of the Lord Chancellor.

Before making these recommendations the Lord Chancellor and the Prime Minister consult other people. It is entirely a matter for them whom they consult but it is doubtful if they would ever make an important judicial appointment without consulting some Supreme Court judges, and the law officers of the Crown or one of them. The Lord Chancellor also consults his Permanent Secretary, who has his ear to the ground and has a pretty good idea of the standard of most barristers who might be considered in the running for a judgeship.

No one applies for appointment as a puisne judge (pronounced " puny ") *i.e.*, High Court judge. He must wait to be invited.

Those who want to become county court judges or stipendiary magistrates may apply to the Lord Chancellor's department for consideration for such appointments. Once again, the Lord Chancellor's Permanent Secretary will know, or make inquiries to enable him to tell the Lord Chancellor, a good deal about the applicants. The Lord Chancellor will no doubt also

[2] The reason for wills, divorces and maritime matters all being grouped in one division is historical. There is going to be a change in this grouping.

ask Supreme Court judges and the law officers or one of them for their opinions.

The Court of Appeal judges, known as Lords Justices of Appeal are often confused with Law Lords. The Lords Justices are not peers, unless by coincidence they happen to be. Most Court of Appeal judges have been promoted from the High Court but occasionally it happens that a barrister is promoted direct from the Bar to the Court of Appeal. The Lord Chief Justice normally presides over the Court of Appeal (Criminal Division) and the Master of the Rolls over the first court in the Civil Division.

Every Supreme Court judge is knighted unless he already has a title taking precedence over knighthood. Now that these judges have increased in number the fact that this honour is granted to them on appointment has been the cause of some criticism. In 1940 there were only thirty-five of them. Now there are more than double that number. It is said that in no other profession is the honour of knighthood bestowed so liberally. Distinguished doctors and other people in important positions, it is said, are not treated anything like so well in this respect.

While one can understand this criticism, it is important that the dignity of the High Court Bench should be upheld and this is one method of doing it. Moreover, until fifteen or twenty years ago, the honour of knighthood was, no doubt, taken into account by a prospective judge as consolation for the fact that between 1830 and 1954 there was no increase in a High Court judge's salary, in spite of the decline in the value of money.

There are, it is true, denigrators of the whole judicial system and people who say that judges think much too much of themselves and that their place in public life should be far lower than it is. Lawyers may be a necessity, they say, but to a great extent they batten on other people's misfortunes. Why are not doctors, who save life and limb, more important than judges who do nothing of the kind? It is impossible for me to deal with such criticisms objectively and I shall not try to do so. Personally I believe that the value of the outstanding services rendered by Supreme Court judges should continue to be recognised as it has been in the past. And, though I see the doctors' point of view, if the tradition of knighting High Court judges were now altered, it would inevitably appear as if they were being downgraded. As an upright Bench is one of our few remaining envied possessions, this would be a pity.

When the Court of Appeal was created in the last century its judges were asked whether they would prefer to have a higher salary than High Court judges or to become members of the Privy Council. They opted to become members of the Privy Council and in the result all members of the Court of Appeal are entitled to the appellation " The Right Honourable."

In addition to the judges mentioned in the Appendix there are the ordinary recorders (as distinct from the full-time recorders of London, Manchester and Liverpool). They are barristers of at least five years' standing, appointed by the Lord Chancellor to preside at borough quarter sessions. Quarter sessions is the court which tries serious but not the most serious criminal cases and which hears appeals from magistrates and has certain civil jurisdiction.

County quarter sessions are presided over by a legally qualified chairman or deputy-chairman and justices. The chairman or deputy-chairman conducts the proceedings and sums up to the jury but the justices as a whole decide on the question of sentence or on the question of an appeal.

At borough quarter sessions the recorder deals with the whole case like any other judge. The remuneration of recorders (other than the three full-time recorders) is small and varies according to the number of inhabitants in the borough where they sit. Most recorders lose money as a result of accepting office.

Their position is a somewhat anomalous one. They are ordinary practising barristers elevated to the Bench four times a year during the sitting of quarter sessions. The system works well and you do not find that A, a barrister who loses a case before B, sitting as recorder, gets his own back on B when the positions are reversed and A is the recorder and B is appearing in front of him. The fact that it doesn't happen like that must stem from the tradition of integrity.

Slightly apropos of that let me tell you of A and B, two well-known county court practitioners who frequently opposed each other and were very doughty fighters. One day they were travelling together to a county court by train. " Are you against me? " asked A of B. " Indeed, yes," said B, who unknown to A had just been appointed the judge of the county court to which they were going.

There are certain judicial officers with whom I shall not deal (*e.g.* masters and different kinds of registrars) as, except for county court registrars, none of them normally tries cases. But the county court registrar regularly tries small cases. From his decision there is an appeal to the judge of the court. County court registrars are solicitors. One reason for this is that they deal with the fixing of the parties' costs. They understand detailed bills of costs, barristers do not. As far as my experience goes, most registrars in the county court try their cases sensibly, fairly and compassionately. Few of them have any pretensions to being great lawyers, but most cases which they try involve questions of fact rather than questions of law. As the jurisdiction of the county court judge has increased, so has the jurisdiction of the registrar and it may be that it will not be long before a registrar will try cases involving up to £100, as recommended by the Beeching Commission.

It has been suggested that county court registrars should be available for promotion to county court judgeships. Although I do not doubt that there are some who would make perfectly reasonable county court judges, I am doubtful if many registrars are sufficiently good lawyers to justify such promotion. But the vital objection to such promotion is the same as the objection to the promotion of solicitors direct to the Bench. The maintenance of the judicial reputation for integrity is of such vital importance that in my view in no circumstances should the sieving process be dispensed with. A registrar is only likely to be known to one or two county court judges and the practitioners in the court or courts where he sits. In my view it is essential that, as far as possible, no one should become a judge unless he is well known to High Court judges and members of the Bar.

It may be said against this that solicitors are available to be appointed as stipendiary magistrates. Personally, for the reasons which I have stated, I don't think they should be, even though they may make very good magistrates. At any rate at the moment there is no likelihood of their promotion to the higher judiciary. Moreover, the fact that the principle to which I have referred has been slightly eroded by the possibility of solicitors becoming stipendiary magistrates is no reason for eroding it still further. But it can be seen from the Beeching Report that there is a real danger that this will happen, unless this consideration of integrity is brought to the fore.

I now come to the background of the 117 judges and magistrates.

Only nine of them have never been married. Fifteen married twice and one three times. The 108 married judges produced altogether 228 children.

Just under two-thirds of the 117 judges disclosed their outside interests. Gardening (23) is the most frequent pursuit, followed by golf (18), fishing (14) and walking (10). Music and shooting (each 9) came next. Travel accounted for eight, tennis for five, sailing, idling and the theatre each for three. Two favoured the Turf, one old coins and, curiously enough, only one cricket.

Ninety out of the 117 served either in the 1914–18 war or the 1939–45 war in the Navy, Army or Air Force. In the later war, five were in the Navy, sixty in the Army and fifteen in the Air Force.

Of the 117, ten had been Members of Parliament and another five, unsuccessful candidates. Thirty-two have written books of one kind or another, though the majority of these were technical, legal works. Sixteen of them were governors of schools, colleges, hospitals or charitable institutions.

I now come to their education and examination records. It is interesting to compare the pattern of the education of today's judges with that of the judges thirty years ago. I looked up the scholastic careers of the thirty-five Court of Appeal and High Court judges sitting when Orwell wrote *England Your England* (1941). It must be remembered that nearly all of them went to school before the turn of the century. Approximately four-fifths of those judges went to public schools and the remainder did not. Winchester easily headed the list with eight, Eton came a bad second with three, Marlborough and Merchant Taylors' each had two and no other school had more than one. Twenty of the judges went to Oxford, six to Cambridge and one to Manchester University. Eight did not go to a university.

By 1969 the number of Court of Appeal and High Court judges had risen to seventy-three. I took a random sample of thirty-six Court of Appeal and High Court judges out of the seventy-three. Of these thirty-six, thirty-one went to public schools. This time Eton, Gresham's School, Holt and Winchester headed the list with three each. The only other school with more than one was Uppingham. By now Oxford had almost lost its ascendancy, seventeen of the judges having gone there and sixteen to Cambridge. One went to Manchester, one went to London and one did not go to a university at all. But the proportion of those going to a university had risen markedly since 1941 and, as will be seen, it continues to rise.

The picture in the House of Lords is much the same. Of the random sample of twelve (out of twenty-four) Law Lords, ten went to public schools and two did not. Eton had two and no other school more than one. Eight went to Oxford and three to Cambridge and one did not go to a university.

My sample was taken in July 1969. Between then and May 1970 four more High Court judges were appointed. Three went to public schools and one did not. Three went to Cambridge and one to Liverpool University.

For the county court judges and stipendiary magistrates I have not taken a comparison with their predecessors of 1940. Of my random sample of forty-five (out of ninety) county court judges thirty-two went to public schools and the remainder did not. Shrewsbury had four; Clifton, Charterhouse, Eton, Haileybury and Winchester each two. No other school had more than one. Oxford and Cambridge were equally divided with twenty each. Two went to Leeds, one to London and two did not go to a university.

Of my random sample of twenty-four stipendiary magistrates (out of a total of forty-eight), twenty went to public schools and the remainder did not. Lancing was top with three, Eton and Harrow had two each and no other school had more than one. For some reason Oxford must like supplying stipendiary magistrates for no less than twelve went there, but only four went to Cambridge, two to London, one to Birmingham and one to Leeds. Four did not go to a university. The overall figures for schools for all judges and magistrates show Eton top with nine, Winchester second with seven, followed by Charterhouse six, Harrow, Lancing and Shrewsbury five, Repton and Uppingham four, Clifton, Cheltenham, Gresham's School, Holt, Haileybury, Marlborough and Rugby three, Fettes, The Leys, Radley, St. Christopher's, Letchworth, St. Paul's and Stoneyhurst two. No other school had more than one. Between July 1969 and May 1970, Charterhouse, Repton, Shrewsbury and Winchester have each added one.

The figures for county court judges and stipendiary magistrates were also as at July 1969. Between then and May 1970 there were twelve new appointments of county court judges and two of stipendiary magistrates. I have not yet found the school of one of the county court judges. Of the remaining eleven, nine went to public schools and two did not. Seven went to Oxford and three to Cambridge, one to Manchester and one to Birmingham University. Of the two stipendiary magistrates, I have not found the school for one. The other did not go to a public school but they both went to Cambridge.

If one takes the overall figure for judges and magistrates from the House of Lords downwards and if one assumes the same type of education for the county court judges and magistrates sitting in 1941 as for Supreme Court judges, it appears that there has been a slight move away from the public schools. In 1941 about four-fifths of the Supreme Court judges had gone to public schools; in 1969, eighty-three out of 117 judges and magistrates had gone to public schools, that is to say about sixteen out of twenty in 1941 as opposed to about sixteen out of twenty-three in 1969.

The period between July 1969 and May 1970 is too short and the appointments made during it are too few to justify any conclusions, but, for what it is worth, it shows no further movement away from the public schools.

The most obvious change since 1940 is the increase in the number of judges going to a university. Of the 135 judges and magistrates sitting in May 1970, only eight had not been to a university compared with eight out of thirty-five in 1941. The bias in favour of Oxford and Cambridge remains. Of the 127 who went to a university, sixty-five went to Oxford and fifty to Cambridge.

It must, however, be remembered that the youngest of all these judges and magistrates was 19 when the 1939 war began and most of them were considerably older. The average age was 60 in 1970 and this means that on average they were about 30 in 1939. It is therefore true to say that all the schools and probably all the universities of these judges were chosen well before the 1939–45 war. Consequently, the lead of Oxford and Cambridge over other universities is not really a true guide to the future pattern. There are now many universities with law schools which did not exist before the last war.

The result of my inquiries can be summed up by saying (1) that up to the 1939–45 war, boys who were potential judges or magistrates mainly went to public schools but that the number of those going to other schools is slightly increasing; (2) that a high proportion of all of them went to a university, usually Oxford or Cambridge; (3) that that high proportion is increasing still further and that almost all potential judges and magistrates go to a university.

It will be ten to twenty years before it will be possible to say whether the slight movement away from the public schools will become greater and whether other universities start to take a bigger place in the career of potential judges and magistrates. I shall be surprised if both these things do not happen. As for schools, thirty-four out of 117 judges did not go to public schools in the years between 1920 and 1933. It would be surprising if this figure were not considerably increased in the future. As for universities, I have visited many of the universities where law is read and I have found the student material of a very high standard.

Judges' records in their final Bar examinations are not outstanding and this should be a comfort to some students. Of forty-eight Law Lords, Lords Justices and High Court judges, only thirteen obtained first-class honours. Of forty-five county court judges only three took first-class honours and of twenty-three stipendiary magistrates none took first-class honours.

Out of twelve Law Lords, three were in the first class, six in the second and three in the third.

The best results were in the Court of Appeal, where out of five Lords Justices three took firsts, one a second and one a third. But a total of only five may do them more than justice. Out of thirty-one High Court judges, seven were in the first class, ten in the second and fourteen in the third.

Out of the total of 116 Law Lords, Lords Justices, High

Court and county court judges and stipendiary magistrates, fifty-seven passed in the third class. (The difference between 116 and 117 is accounted for by the fact that one magistrate was a solicitor and therefore took no Bar examinations.)

The matter of examinations is important. For over 150 years after 1700, no Bar examinations were taken by prospective barristers. There was a " students' box " or " cribbe " in court which they regularly attended, and afterwards they could talk to counsel, and sometimes the judges, about the cases. They also took part in moots (mock trials on questions of law). Then they followed barristers from court to court, dined in Hall with them and the Benchers [3] and finally, when it was considered that they had acquired sufficient legal knowledge, they were duly called to the Bar. Judges then as now were chosen from the Bar and during that period we had some of the finest judges that we have had in English legal history. So the system appears to have worked well, but no doubt it relied on the fact that most barristers first studied law at a university. That was where they acquired their theoretical knowledge.

In 1852 the system was changed on a voluntary basis and some twenty years later Bar examinations were made compulsory. There is a movement to make the examinations more practical, but the disadvantage of having examinations at all is that students have become more and more divorced from barristers, benchers and judges.

In the old days dining in Hall had real value for the student, as he could discuss with his seniors cases which he had heard and he could learn about the profession from the practical side. Today students still have to eat dinners, and this has

[3] The ruling body of each Inn of Court are called Masters of the Bench or Benchers. They mainly consist of judges and senior barristers.

some value because they meet each other. But unfortunately, as their examinations are otherwise provided for, too little attention is given to the students by the senior members of the Inns of Court. Consequently students complain at the necessity of eating dinners and say that they never meet anyone except fellow students. It is true that there are week-ends at Cumberland Lodge in Great Windsor Park where students mix with barristers, benchers and judges. This contact is invaluable and during the week-ends there are lectures and informal discussions worth infinitely more than most examinations. But there is only room for a limited number of students and each Inn only has three week-ends every two years, so that very few students in all can have the benefit of them. But it is this kind of thing on a far larger scale that is needed, *e.g.* regular discussions between barristers, benchers and students after dinner in Hall. And a revival of the " students' box " would be no bad thing.

A movement has been started for newly-called barristers to be attached to county court judges to learn something of the practical side of county court litigation. One county court judge has had the excellent idea of letting them spend a week in the county court office under the tutelage of the chief clerk and the bailiffs. In the result they must learn a good deal more about the inner workings of the county court than a judge at present knows when he first starts to sit. It might well be an advantage if every prospective county court judge spent a week with the clerks and bailiffs of a county court.

I should say a word about High Court judges going on circuit. The most amusing description of this is to be found in the late Cyril Hare's *Tragedy at Law*. Cyril Hare was in fact a county court judge, His Honour Judge Gordon Clark. It was very sad that he died only a few years after his promotion to the Bench. *Tragedy at Law* is a classic and it is likely to be read as long as there is a legal profession in England.

When a High Court judge goes on circuit he lives in lodgings which are specially provided for him. He has a young barrister with him who is known as a marshal and who acts as a sort of tame secretary. Wives sometimes accompany the judges and this depends upon whether the senior judge invites them. Today he usually does. When the wives do go, the wife of the senior judge takes command of the ladies, occasionally with devastating effect. It has been said that one particular wife took command of the judge as well. This may well have been true, except, it is to be hoped, for his decisions in court.

The judge receives a small allowance per day out of which he has to pay his cost of living, including the wages of the butler, the cook, etc. If the judge's wife accompanies him, he has to pay for her too. The allowance varies according to the number of judges who have to be catered for and it is an understatement to say it hardly covers a judge's expenses.

Many people do not know how to write to judges or address them when they meet, if they are strangers. I have set out the rules in the appendix but I'll mention one now. An ordinary recorder is called " Sir " in court, full-time recorders " My Lord." When I first appeared in front of an ordinary recorder, I was unable to find out how he should be addressed and, of course, mine would be the first case to be called on. The only recorder before whom I had previously appeared was the Recorder of London and he, of course, was called My Lord. So I took no chances and called an ordinary recorder My Lord, but he answered just the same. It was prophetic, as later he became a High Court judge.

Judges receive a number of threatening letters and also

letters of gratitude. Occasionally it has been necessary to provide police protection for a judge or his wife as a result of some such threats but there has been no case of anyone assaulting or attempting to assault the judge or his wife or family. On the whole regular criminals seem to appreciate that a judge has a duty to do. One hardened criminal told me that in his opinion Lord Goddard (who was anything but a weak judge) was the fairest judge in all England.

On the whole, prisoners do not seem to dislike judges particularly. Here are a few selections of their opinions:

" Yes, he was fair all right—the rotten old bastard."

" I thought he dealt with me leniently, but he was a pig the way he did it."

" He was lenient as he could be with me. I suppose I was lucky."

" I don't think he was really with it, as he never looked at me but kept his head down all the time. He might have been more lenient if he had bothered to read the probation officer's report."

" From what he had heard about me he was very fair. I had twelve months and I expected three years. He had a little chuckle when he sentenced me—he had a sense of humour. I was also chuckling when he said ' Twelve months '."

This brings me to the public image of the modern judge. Though judges as a whole come well out of my researches, there are complaints. It is only a small minority of judges who give rise to these complaints but unfortunately the good judge is not news, the bad judge is; like the man who bit the dog.

" The main thing wrong with the English judge and for that matter any judge," writes a schoolboy, " is that he is only human."

How right he is. On one occasion a litigant in my court, whose case was going to be tried by another judge, said: " If the judge makes that order, it won't be justice."

" Who ever told you you were going to get justice here? " I asked.

" But I thought—" he began.

" I know," I said. " You thought you'd come to a Court of Justice. So you have. But it's a court of *human* justice. We do our best but, if you are in the right, it does not necessarily mean that you will succeed. You probably will, but we are only human and make mistakes."

Strangely enough he fully understood this.

If the only complaint which could justifiably be made against judges were that they were only human, they would not be. There are, no doubt, judges who, though occasionally mistaken, never fall below the high standard of judicial behaviour which they adopted from the moment of their appointment. But not all can maintain this high standard.

It is right that a judge's conduct should be subject to public and private criticism, but it is not always remembered that no judge may reply to such criticism. If something which he has said is misreported, he may refer to the matter in open court, but that is all he may do and, when people write to *The Times* complaining about his conduct, he does not write a letter of explanation. There is no law to prevent him from doing this, but it is traditional that he should not and tradition plays a very big part in the English judicial system.

The tradition of wrapping up judges in scarlet and ermine and horsehair may tend to obscure the fact that they are, as the schoolboy said, only human beings but I think it is quite useful to give a judge a sort of impersonal look. I am sure

that the litigants at Willesden County Court took more notice
of me in wig and robe than if I had simply worn a lounge suit.
I also suspect that, if you put the prisoners walking round the
exercise yard at Wandsworth prison into judicial robes and
sat them on the Bench, everyone would think how learned they
looked.   Conversely, if you took all the members of the Court
of Appeal, put them into prison uniform and walked them
round Wandsworth prison yard, visitors would note their
near-set eyes, receding chins and low foreheads.

In describing the public image of the judge I must deal
with the complaints of abuse of power, remoteness and lack of
imagination which I have mentioned earlier.   But before I deal
with these complaints I think it only fair to the judges as a
whole to refer to some of the more favourable statements which
I have received about them.

Earlier I mentioned the view of a student who had visited
the assizes and thought he detected bias on the part of the
judge.   Here is the remainder of what he said.

" Until I visited the assizes recently I had a very set idea
of what a judge was like, a senile old man dressed in his
magnificent robes and with all the majesty he could
muster, taking hardly any part in the proceedings except
when the prosecution or the defence raised an objection
to the other's questioning of a witness.   The judge would
merely answer ' Objection overruled ' or ' Objection
sustained.'   At the end of the case he would sum up the
prosecution and defence's case with the utmost impartiality
and fairness.   I have found now that this attitude is
completely wrong.   For a start ' Objection overruled '
and ' Objection sustained ' are Americanisms, but many
people believe that they are used in English courts.   In
fact so far as my experience has shown, judges are entirely

human and take an active part in the proceedings. If he thinks that a point needs bringing out or needs clarification he tells the questioner or witness in no uncertain terms."

Then he added the passage about bias (page 6).

Some of those who have written to me derive their knowledge solely from fictional sources. They have never been in court or seen a judge, but the views which they have formed show that the main fictional media, television, cinema, theatre and novels do not seem to denigrate the British judiciary, though sometimes they obviously give a wrong impression of their role.

Here is the view of someone who knows judges at first hand. This comes from the chief crime reporter of a national newspaper.

" My personal observation is that in their own quiet way judges are trying to keep abreast with the modern world. What must impress is the desire of judges while sitting to speak in as simple and plain language as can be understood by all. Judges operate in a world far removed from all but the few who get caught up in the wheels of justice, and therefore changes take longer to be noticed but I personally believe that behind all the trappings of ancient ceremonies which surround the judiciary the men who sit in judgment have on the whole been moving with the times, in fact some judges who have been involved in major criminal trials recently have been doing more than their fair share in seeing that improvements to the system are carried out."

I shall end this lecture with the opinion of a schoolboy:

" There is something warmly patriotic surrounding the whole of the British judicial system, an aura of friendliness coupled with a sense of fair play and reason. It seems as though the whole paraphernalia of justice in this country has been proudly handed down from Plantagenet knights to the young of today. One almost feels that the wigs and robes of the judge and his clerks and barristers, etc., had been peeled off the backs of dusty museum figures and placed over the wrinkled but still firm and resolute features of the court players who, decked out in their newly hired costumes file into the court room to begin another scene, maybe with different lines but still in the same play, ' Justice will be done.' But however much the actors improvise and toy with words, the crux of the plot centres on the lead character, the judge. It is he who has the best though fewest words, who directs and produces the play and has the final summing-up in the tense last scene. It is he who sits above the rest—old, wise, like an owl blinking at the bright flashy lights of the modern reckless-ness and brashness that he sees brought before him each day. And when all the animals of the wood bring before him their squabbles to resolve, he, perched above them on his branch, pauses a minute and refers to his past experi-ence and then gives his decision, which no one except the noisiest and cockiest young animal ever questions. But the judge does not stand entirely alone, he is backed up by the whole English legal system which is or at any rate seems, the epitome of all that is fair and just and, not meaning to be snide, British."

The interesting thing about this attractive piece of prose is that the author was just 15 when he wrote it.

APPENDIX

1. TABLE OF PRECEDENCE [4] OF THE JUDGES WITH THE QUALIFICATIONS FOR THEIR APPOINTMENTS AND THEIR SALARIES

JUDGE	QUALIFICATION FOR APPOINTMENT	SALARY
Lord High Chancellor	None	£14,500
Lord Chief Justice of England	Barrister of 15 years' standing or judge of the High Court	£14,250
Lords of Appeal in Ordinary	Barrister of 15 years' standing or judge of the High Court [5]	£13,000
Master of the Rolls	Barrister of 15 years' standing or judge of the High Court	£13,000
President of the Probate, Divorce and Admiralty Division	Barrister of 15 years' standing or judge of the High Court	£13,000
Lords Justices of Appeal	Barrister of 15 years' standing or judge of the High Court	£11,500
High Court Judges	Barrister of 10 years' standing	£11,500
Vice-Chancellor of the County Palatine of Lancaster	Barrister of 10 years' standing	Between £6,550 and £11,500
Official Referee	Barrister of 10 years' standing	£6,800
Recorder of London	Barrister of 10 years' standing	£9,000
The Common Serjeant	Barrister of 10 years' standing	£8,000
The 10 additional judges of the Central Criminal Court	Barrister of 10 years' standing	£7,500
Recorders of Liverpool and Manchester	Barrister of 10 years' standing	£7,400
The judge of the Mayor's and City of London Court	Barrister of 7 years' standing	£6,750
Full-time Chairman and Deputy-Chairman of Quarter Sessions	Barrister or solicitor of 10 years' standing	£6,550–£7,200
County Court judges	Barrister of 7 years' standing	£6,550

[4] There is no certainty about the order of precedence of judges after the Vice-Chancellor of the County Palatine of Lancaster.

[5] Or the equivalent in Scotland or Northern Ireland.

Stipendiary and Metropolitan Magistrates	Barrister of 7 years' standing	£5,300– £6,350
Judge of the Court of Passage of Liverpool	Barrister of 7 years' standing	£2,500
Judge of the Court of Record for the Hundred of Salford	Barrister of 10 years' standing	£1,000
Chancellor of the County Palatine Court of Durham	No statutory qualification but normally filled by a Chancery Q.C.	£400 per annum plus £30 for each day of sitting

There are one or two other courts, *e.g.* in Norwich and Bristol, but neither they nor the Liverpool Court of Passage, the County Palatine Court of Durham or the Salford Court of Record are likely to survive the implementation of the Beeching Report.

2. PENSIONS

The Lord Chancellor receives a pension of £6,250 a year. The pensions of the other judges are regulated by complicated rules. These are far too detailed and intricate to be stated here, but the following rules for the pensions of county court judges will be a rough guide to the pensions of other judges. If you want to know the pension of any particular type of retired judge, the only sure way of finding out is to ask one.

The full pension for married county court judges is half their final year's salary; if unmarried the amount is two-thirds. The reason for a married judge receiving less than an unmarried judge is because the widow's pension is partly provided for in this way. They must have served at least fifteen years on the Bench to earn the full pension. If they retire on the ground of ill-health before reaching retiring age and before completing fifteen years' service, they will get a proportion of the full pension graduated according to the number of years which they have served. Similarly, if, as they are entitled to do, they retire at the age of 65 without having completed fifteen years' service, they will get a proportion of the full pension. Any judge who retires before the age of 65 without having completed fifteen years' service will get no pension at all unless his retirement is on the ground of ill-health. A county court judge cannot retire on pension before the age of 65 except on the ground of ill-health, however many years he may have completed. (A High Court judge may retire at any age on full pension provided he has completed fifteen years' service.)

Judges' widows receive one-sixth of the judge's last salary. And, where there is a widow with children under 16 years, the children receive one-twelfth of the judge's salary in addition until they reach the age of 16. If there is no widow the children receive one-sixth.

In addition, a married judge on retirement will receive free of tax a lump sum equal to half of one year's salary; if unmarried the amount is two-thirds. If the judge dies before retirement, his widow will receive the lump sum which he would have received had he lived and retired on the day of his death. If he has already completed fifteen years' service on the day of his death, she will get the maximum sum. If he has not completed fifteen years, she will get the amount which he would have received had he retired on the day of his death on the ground of ill-health.

3. ROBES

1. The Lord Chancellor wears a black damask and gold embroidered robe which costs about £1,300. He always wears a full-bottomed wig which costs about £75.

2. On ceremonial occasions the Lord Chief Justice wears a robe of scarlet and ermine with a train. The Master of the Rolls, the Lords Justices and the President of the Probate, Divorce and Admiralty Division wear a robe similar to that of the Lord Chancellor. On ordinary occasions in court, however, the Lord Chief Justice wears the same robe as a Queen's Bench judge if sitting as judge of the Queen's Bench Division or as a Lord Justice if sitting in the Court of Appeal. The Master of the Rolls, the Lords Justices, the President of the Probate, Divorce and Admiralty Division and the Chancery judges wear the same kind of morning coat and waistcoat and the same gown as is worn by a Q.C. on ceremonial occasions. The cost of this outfit is about £115.

The Queen's Bench judges have four sets of robes: a winter criminal robe, which is scarlet and ermine; a winter civil robe which is black and ermine; a summer criminal robe which is scarlet and silk and a summer civil robe which is black and silk. The total cost of these is about £1,500.

The county court judge has a purple and silk robe (with a hood which is worn on ceremonial occasions) and the cost is about £85.

The Recorder of London wears a special red robe rather like that of a High Court judge. The other judges of the Central Criminal Court and of quarter sessions wear the morning coat and waistcoat and Q.C.'s gown referred to above. The Common Serjeant has a special black ceremonial robe as well.

All judges have to have a full-bottomed wig for use on ceremonial occasions but in court they wear a bench wig. This costs about £50.

Many High Court judges buy their robes second-hand from retired judges.

4. HOW TO ADDRESS JUDGES

Law Lords are addressed like any other peer, *e.g.* The Right
Honourable Lord X. And in writing to or speaking to them
you will call them Lord X. Lords Justices of Appeal are
always knights unless they happen to be peers or baronets. In
writing to them formally at the Law Courts you would address
them as The Right Honourable Lord Justice X, but rarely
do people outside the legal profession write to Lords Justices
on a formal matter. Normally they will be writing to a Lord
Justice in his personal capacity and in that case they will
address the letter to The Right Honourable Sir George X and,
according to whether they know him or not, they will address
him inside the letter Dear Sir George, or Dear Sir. When
meeting him they will call him Sir George. A similar rule
applies to High Court judges who are also always knights,
unless they happen to be peers or baronets. A formal letter
addressed to them at the Law Courts would be addressed to
The Honourable Mr. Justice X but anyone writing to them
personally would write Dear Sir George or Dear Sir and
would address the envelope to The Honourable Sir George
X. When you see Smith J. in a law report, it means Mr.
Justice Smith.

There is some doubt as to the extent to which High Court
judges are entitled to the appellation The Honourable. I
think that the better view is that they are entitled to it as long
as they are actually High Court judges, though it has been
claimed that they are only entitled to The Honourable in
conjunction with the title Mr. Justice. I think that this
restriction is wrong and that, as long as a High Court judge
is in office, he is entitled to be called either The Honourable
Mr. Justice X or The Honourable Sir George X. As soon,
however, as he retires, he ceases to be entitled to be called

The Honourable. Barristers always call a judge either in
writing to him or addressing him out of court, Judge or Lord
Justice, as the case may be. In court, High Court judges and
above are called My Lord, county court judges Your Honour.
There is at the moment only one woman High Court judge
and she is known as The Honourable Mrs. Justice Lane or
The Honourable Dame Elizabeth Lane. In court she is called
My Lady.

The really difficult one is the Official Referee. He is a
minor judge in the High Court who tries cases involving great
detail, *e.g.* builders' claims or cases involving complicated
accounts. He is entitled to the appellation His Honour and in
court he is called Your Honour. When you write to him
officially or unofficially you will call him His Honour George X.
He is in fact senior in precedence to county court judges but
he does not have the title Judge. So when you introduce him,
can you call him anything except Mr.? It is no use pretending
that most people don't like titles. They do. And it seems
rather bad luck on an Official Referee, who is senior to a
county court judge, that a county court judge should be called
Judge and the Official Referee Mr.

The same problem arises with a county court judge who
has retired. While he holds his office, a county court judge
is known as His Honour Judge X, and when you write to him
or speak to him you call him Judge X or simply Judge. When
he retires, he ceases to be entitled to be known as Judge. He
is simply His Honour George X, just like an Official Referee.
In the case of a retired county court judge the problem is often
dealt with by people who knew him as a judge still calling him
Judge. The only alternative is Mr. because you can't call a
county court judge or an Official Referee out of court, Your
Honour. But, although an Official Referee is in fact a judge,

he is never called Judge so, for members of the public, I can see no alternative but to introduce him as Mr. X.

As far as members of the Bar are concerned, I think the problem could be solved by calling him Judge, just as they would call a High Court or county court judge. To call him Official Referee is too much of a mouthful, he is in fact a judge and, as I have said, senior in precedence to county court judges. That being so, it seems to my mind a simple solution, though I don't know whether anybody else has arrived at it. When I wrote a book called *Brief to Counsel*, which was supposed to be an introduction to the Bar, I approached this problem and ended up by saying that the best thing for a young barrister to do was not to talk to Official Referees as I did not know how to address them.

Stipendiary magistrates are referred to in court by people outside the legal profession as Your Worship but advocates, whether solicitors or barristers, who are experienced in these matters always call him Sir. Outside court he has no title, except for the Chief Metropolitan magistrate, who is normally knighted. The same rule applies to justices but sometimes it may be known that the Chairman of the Bench, particularly if he happens to be the Mayor, likes to be called Your Worship by everyone, including advocates.

Full-time chairmen or deputy-chairmen of quarter sessions are now entitled to be called His Honour Judge.

CHAPTER 2

PUBLIC IMAGE OF THE JUDGES

More opinions about judges—the Communist view—the status of irremovability—judicial abuse of power—solicitors occasionally criticised unfairly—jokes in court—private interviews between judge and counsel—a scandalous case—should judges have a trial run before appointment?—a sabbatical year on appointment?—the judges' rules—the effect of a case upon third parties.

I SHALL start by continuing with other people's comments about judges.

Both sides of industry give the judge a good character. A distinguished trade unionist has an enormous admiration for judges and has been " impressed and struck not only with the justice they dispense but with their fairness and helpfulness in seeking to establish the truth." While from the management side comes the comment that judges are human and subject to the frailties of human nature but that their ability and integrity must always be undoubted.

From the Communist point of view the whole judicial system is wrong, as it exists as part of a legal system whose principal aim is the preservation of capitalist property relations. The Editor of the *Morning Star* writes:

" I think it is generally accepted that most High Court judges are drawn from ruling-class circles. Some years ago I saw an analysis of the judges at the time in the House of Lords and Court of Appeal and the High Court, which revealed that 85 per cent. of them went to public schools or private day schools and only 15 per cent. were educated at grammar schools controlled by local authorities. I think it was Sergeant Sullivan Q.C. who wrote in his memoirs that the English Bench ' is exclusively composed of men who have grown up in the artificial atmosphere of the ruling class, the public school, the university, the well-provided apprenticeship to the Inns of Court, the lucrative practice and the accumulation of wealth. None have ever suffered that excellent corrective of theoretical opinion, hunger for the price of a meal.' It is therefore natural that on the whole judges should reflect the outlook, opinions and prejudices of the employing or capitalist class rather than the working class. However, judges are also affected by the general climate of opinion and have had to take into account the growth and influence of the organised working class and labour movement. While the significance of their independence of the ' executive government ' can be exaggerated, there have been occasions when they have taken decisions to protect the liberty of the subject from encroachments by the executive. But again I do not think that this affects the main point, which is that the judges are part of the state apparatus of capitalism and of a legal system designed to ensure its perpetuation."

Undoubtedly public schools have played a large part in providing the judiciary of the last hundred years. And, on the whole, they seem to have done a very good job. I wonder if any Communist country has judges who, whatever their faults, are people of the utmost integrity and generally accepted by every section of the population as being so. If the public schools are partly responsible for this standard of integrity it is not a bad advertisement. And I notice that not the slightest suggestion, express or implied, is made by the Editor of the

Morning Star, in his fair and moderate statement, against the personal integrity of English judges.

Many of my correspondents do not refer to the pomp and ceremonies of the law, but of those who do the majority approve of them. Quite a number, however, do not, and consider that they are out of place in a modern democratic age. A few suggested that their object is mainly to bolster up the judge's already too high opinion of himself. Some of these criticisms come from people who have never attended court. It is once again difficult for me to speak objectively on this subject. I dare say my already too high opinion of myself was increased by wearing my wig and robe and by the voice of the usher shouting, when I came into court, " Silence " or " Be Uncovered in Court "; not that any man ever had his hat on. All the same I think that, provided judges have good manners and try to prevent those appearing in front of them from being overawed by the procedure, these trappings are an advantage and help to maintain the dignity and impersonality of the law.

Two schoolboys refer to the status of irremovability of a High Court judge.

The first writes:

" The judiciary has changed in recent years. Gone is the artificiality of the Bench, the octogenarian judge, the impossibility of a woman judge. A marked trend has been the genuine desire of senior judges to adapt the law to modern needs. The position of the judge is very secure indeed. He can only be removed by an address by the two Houses of Parliament. It may be argued that our judiciary is not perfect enough for such security. In my opinion there is little to complain about. So even if we

do kill all the lawyers, there is no need to tamper with
Her Majesty's judges as well."
And the second:
" Perhaps one disadvantage of the present system is that
once a man becomes a judge he is more or less secure in
his position and he can only be removed by joint recommendation of both Houses of Parliament. Thus if a man
got into the position of a judge and turned out to be a
thoroughly villainous character or became senile or in
any other way had his fair judgment impaired and was not
too closely scrutinised he could work havoc with justice,
but this is a minor criticism. This would not happen very
often."

Dr. Johnson said much the same thing when advocating
the compulsory retirement of judges on the death of the
Sovereign. " A judge may be corrupt," he said, " but there
may be no evidence to prove it." He said this in 1760 when the
tradition of incorruptibility had not been sufficiently established. This tradition started with the Act of Settlement of
1700, which for the first time gave judges complete independence of the Crown and the Government. The Act, by providing
that only Parliament itself could apply for the removal of a
High Court judge, ensured (a) that there was in the last resort
a power to remove, *e.g.* a villainous judge, and (b) that that
power could not be abused. Thereafter judges really could
decide cases " without fear or favour " and it is this independence which was largely the reason for the resulting integrity.

I know of no case of a sitting judge becoming senile. In
fact some judges, still fully capable of doing the work, volun-
tarily resigned, lest the public might become suspicious of their
powers owing to their age. One judge, Mr. Justice Stephen,
was affected by a mental illness and resigned after a leading

article in *The Times* suggested that he should. This was in 1891.

I have already pointed out that Parliament has traditionally held that an address cannot be moved to the Sovereign asking for a judge's removal except on the ground of moral delinquency or incapacitating illness. Unendurable interruptions or gross bad manners are not enough. The lesser judges, official referees, chairmen and deputy-chairmen of quarter sessions, county court judges, stipendiary magistrates and justices can with one qualification be removed by the Lord Chancellor in his discretion. The qualification is that the professional judges can only be removed for " inability or misbehaviour."

But, although High Court judges cannot be removed except on the grounds of moral delinquency, the influence of the Press and of the legal profession as a whole should today be sufficiently persuasive to secure the resignation of a judge who is for one reason or another incapable of discharging his duties to the satisfaction of anyone except himself. It must also be remembered that it is the independence of judges and their security on the Bench that has been a great factor in producing judges of the highest integrity. This tremendous advantage, in my opinion, outweighs the admitted disadvantage that a judge who keeps his inadequacies within certain bounds cannot be removed.

A legal editor says that " the widely held view amongst solicitors about High Court judges is that their level of probity and competence is as high now as it ever was in the past (if not higher), but there is a certain lack of touch with the common man and in consequence absence of appreciation of many of the problems which he faces."

From the Police Federation comes the comment:

" allowing for those who sometimes under pressure of

work appear to allow their personal feelings to overcome their professional impartiality, judges and stipendiary magistrates provoke nothing but admiration from us. It is sometimes necessary to criticise the courts for tending to concentrate more on seeking for excuses for the anti-social behaviour of a criminal than on the suffering caused to his victim or on the protection of society. If the community is to be expected to maintain proper standards of conduct, the judiciary should set an example by passing sentences which adequately reflect society's condemnation of delinquency and in particular its condemnation of the use of violence in the pursuit of crime.''

A schoolboy refers to what was probably a county court case which he attended:

" A great deal of criticism is thrown at the feet of the English judge. He is accused of making personal comments on cases which have no relation to the evidence and, as when wearing their robes and wigs, they tend to look older than their years, it is also their misfortune to be called old-fashioned and out of touch with our modern society. Personally I don't hold with these criticisms, because the judge does in fact see aspects of our society in a far clearer light than the average layman. He must in many cases use a great deal of discretion in dealing with disputes between private individuals and sometimes in criminal cases. I have personally seen this when my parents were taken to court over the pruning of a rather offensive lime tree which overhangs the bottom section of our garden. On having been asked to prune the tree, the owner flatly refused to do so, so I pruned it for him, taking a considerable number of branches off and religiously depositing them at the bottom of his garden.

We were accused of making the tree an eyesore by having unscrupulously removed most of the branches, which was perfectly true. The judge must have realised that, although we were in fact guilty, the tree prevented us from cultivating the bottom of our garden. He awarded a shilling damages. This makes me think that judges are very shrewd men."

A comment from someone acquainted with courts and judges is:

" A judge is a prisoner of his own tradition, which he is very reluctant to criticise for fear of damaging the system which has stood up pretty well over the years. There is a great deal of misunderstanding about him functionally but he may not realise this. Some of the humour expressed by the judge in court implies to many laymen that the average judge is rather a humourless, cold fish. My own limited experience, however, shows that some of these remarks resulting in genuine laughter in court are not necessarily meant to be funny as such, but to help reduce tension, not least for the poor chap in the dock. Then there is the outward manifestation; the wig, the robes, etc. I suppose this is all right if it is what the customer wants and contributes to the dignity and majesty of the law. One judge told me that he felt a proper Charley with his little bouquet to ward off gaol fever."

A well-known journalist and writer says that he is sure that he speaks for a good many journalistic colleagues in saying that the present generation of High Court judges is more esteemed than any in living memory. There is a general belief, he says, that county court judges are wasted and even underworked and that their jurisdiction should be increased still further. " Generally," he says, " High Court judges and stipendiary magistrates enjoy the confidence of nearly all sectors of the public."

An editor writes that judges and stipendiary magistrates are taken for granted and that their integrity is never in question.

" Everyone looks on them as the guardians of human liberty. Occasionally they may err, but usually this can be put right by a higher court. Perhaps he is a bit aloof from ordinary workaday life, but this is not necessarily a bad thing. By and large we regard him as humane, understanding, with a far greater insight of human frailties and cupidity than might appear to some people. His grasp of complex issues and ability to present them simply to a jury is an endless source of wonderment. The British judge deserves to be the envy of the world."

Another editor says that in his opinion the average modern judge is shrewd, utterly honest, mostly compassionate and tolerant of human failings, except where sexual immorality is concerned. " He tends also to be prejudiced against news-papers."

Personally I found the Press on the whole highly responsible and most helpful. And I must say that I thought that most judges, whether they were of the same opinion or not, normally said the same thing in public. If the suggestion that the judge may say something in public which he did not fully mean horrifies anyone, I must point out that this is sometimes almost unavoidable if a judge does not want to hurt someone's feelings unnecessarily.

A judge sometimes has cases, the result of which depends on whether he believes the chief witness on one side or the chief witness on the other. In rejecting the evidence of the one

witness a judge will often say: "I do not think that Mr. So-
and-So was deliberately intending to mislead me but I prefer
the account of the interview given to me by the other witness."
Now the judge may *think* that the witness, whose evidence he
is rejecting, *was* deliberately intending to mislead him, but it
isn't necessary for the purpose of the case for him to say so.
He need only say that, having regard to the probabilities, he
prefers the evidence of the other witness. But sometimes he
will add—not very truthfully—some such words of comfort as
I have mentioned above. If he does this, he does it because he
knows that it is always possible that his view is mistaken,
however strongly he may have formed it.   Why therefore
blacken the witness's character unnecessarily? Most losing
parties will go away from the court slightly happier if they
merely lose the case without also being called unmitigated
liars.

   If a judge has formed the opinion that a man is a liar and
it is necessary for the purposes of his judgment to say so, of
course he must say so. But most judges are aware of their
limitations and of the possibility that they are mistaken and so
they do not call witnesses liars unless it is necessary.

   On one occasion a judge rejected the evidence of a defendant
and her six witnesses and found in favour of the plaintiff who
relied solely on his own evidence. Any lawyer could have told
that the judge disbelieved the defendant and her witnesses,
but in his judgment the judge ascribed their "mistaken
recollection" to a lapse of time. This was a family dispute
and no doubt the judge did not want to exacerbate the situation. This case was a good example of the fact that in coming
to a decision judges don't count heads but weigh the value of
the evidence.

   From a group of prison chaplains comes the comment:

" Judges are often mistaken, sometimes imprudent, occasionally stupid, but always incorrupt and incorruptible."

These quotations are a fair sample of those I have received but, of course, I have had others far less complimentary and, I fear, sometimes for good reason.

The British Legal Association complains about oppressive practices on the part of some judges.

" From time to time," the Association writes, " solicitors fall below the high standard of behaviour required of them and it is necessary for judges to reprimand them in public. Far too frequently certain judges reach hasty conclusions without having heard any explanation from the solicitor concerned. It is submitted that, if a solicitor is about to be criticised, he should be notified privately in advance by the judge, he should be requested to explain his conduct and given an immediate right of reply either in person or by counsel. The Association entirely agrees that judges should be entitled to reprimand solicitors as and when necessary and is simply asking for fair play."

I shall deal with this criticism in detail a little later on.

Another legal editor, rather less emphatically, says the same thing when he refers to the attitude towards solicitors which has been observed in some judges as soon as they are appointed to the Bench.

" I have the feeling," he says, " that it is akin to the rebellion of sons towards their fathers once they are no longer dependent upon them. On the other hand," he goes on, " there seems to be much more courtesy and patience towards them than there used to be."

This leads me to the complaint of abuse of power which started with the allegation of " cutting remarks and quips." As another schoolboy writes:

" In his summing-up, the judge can make scathing remarks about the character of the defendant which could be as damaging as any sentence imposed. It would appear that judges have more or less absolute power in this respect.

Appeal to a higher court would not undo the damage."
Every sane person abuses his power from time to time, but a judge has many more opportunities of doing this than most other people. One unfair remark by one judge can bring the judiciary as a whole into disrepute, just as a few unruly and bad-mannered students can give the young people of today a bad name. In each case the percentage is tiny but the harm is done just the same.

The judge is in a unique position. Not merely is everything said by him during a case absolutely privileged, but he cannot be shouted down as in Parliament, or even answered back if he refuses to allow it. He can cause great misery and frustration to parties, witnesses and advocates. The harm that a judge can do is not merely in actual injustices, that is, wrong decisions, but in sending litigants (and advocates) away with a feeling that their cases have not been properly tried.

The public puts great trust in our judges and, on the whole, this trust is not abused. But a few judges do occasionally say wounding and hurtful things to or about witnesses, counsel or solicitors and the person concerned usually has no remedy. Such remarks may have a permanent effect upon a man, who may be so upset by the unfair strictures upon him that he proceeds to take it out of the next person available, probably his wife. It is hardly too far-fetched to say that the possible chain-reaction from bad behaviour by a judge could be a divorce.

In fact one very important government department was indebted to a county court judge for supplying it with a brilliant young man who subsequently became its chief legal adviser. He came back from a county court hurt and angry and said that nothing would induce him to remain in a profession where he could be treated as he had been by a county court judge. He applied for the civil service job at once and was warmly welcomed.

A well-known journalist, writing of a divorce case where the judge called the wife " stupid in many ways " and a window-cleaner " utterly uncultured," queried whether such remarks were really necessary for the judge's decision. Without knowing all the facts of the case, it is impossible to say whether the remarks were necessary. They may have been, but undoubtedly from time to time judges do make hurtful statements about people when it is not necessary to do so.

One reason for judges making such statements in their judgments is that nearly every judgment is given *ex tempore*, with the result that the judge does not have sufficient time to consider the proper language to use. In consequence he may say things about someone which, on maturer reflection, he would probably have phrased in another manner. On one occasion, for example, a judge, sentencing a woman to a year's suspended imprisonment, described her as a " worthless woman." She was a married woman living with her husband and two children and, though she may have had many serious faults, it is difficult to think that the criticism was justified. Indeed there must be very few people in the world of whom it could be said truly that they were " worthless." It may be that, as the judge was not sending the woman to prison, he decided to punish her by the use of language. No doubt this may be a proper course to take where the language used is suitably chosen, but judges who have the power to hurt people with impunity should use that power, as most of them do, with discretion. I have no doubt that, while I was a judge, I offended in this respect from time to time, but I should certainly have offended less if I had been warned (as I later suggest judges should be warned) about the danger.

Then what justification was there for the judge who, when a prisoner was acquitted, said to the acquitted man in public: " You are discharged. I think you are very lucky in your jury.''? A judge has no business to vent in public his private feelings of indignation at what he considers (very likely correctly) a wrong verdict. The man had been acquitted and in spite of it the judge suggested that he was guilty. This was in fact said before the 1939–45 war by a Lord Chief Justice. And he was the Lord Chief Justice who was a party to a scandalous decision to which I shall be referring later in this lecture.

One of the troubles is that, whether through fear or admiration or for some other reason, most members of the public regard a judge as a very special person. He is treated in court with a subservience and flattery which probably obtains nowhere else and, as he probably gets a similar kind of treatment outside court, it isn't good for some of us.

A judge has to learn to control his adrenal glands and if he is not able to control them, he should not be appointed to the Bench. There have, unfortunately, been too many examples in the last few years to justify the complaint of the British Legal Association. Judges have made adverse remarks about solicitors which were not justified and have later had to withdraw them. What has happened in most of these cases is this. A bad mistake appeared to have been made by a solicitor. The judge was so incensed at what he was told that he castigated the solicitor in strong language. Naturally the Press reported it. The solicitor, who was not present in court, had a perfect answer to the complaint. The next day it was duly given and the judge apologised. But some people who had heard the judge's castigation may not have heard or read of his withdrawal and a grave injustice may therefore have been done to the solicitor.

It is extraordinary that a judge who has been brought up on the principle that no decision should be given until both parties have had the opportunity of being heard should violate this principle. These are the exceptional cases, but, as I have said, it is the exceptional case which gets into the Press and which justifies adverse comment, although it reflects unfairly on the Bench as a whole.

Can nothing be done to prevent this? I think it can and shall shortly suggest a change in the method of appointment of judges. The suggested change is based on the fact that in some cases today the Lord Chancellor cannot sufficiently tell what a judge is going to be like on the Bench until after his appointment.

Some years ago a barrister was appointed to the High Court Bench. He had been a very fierce, able and determined advocate at the Bar and some people were afraid that he might carry his advocacy to the Bench. It is lamentable when this happens. Such judges make up their minds at an early stage and proceed to conduct the case on one party's behalf thereafter, with appalling results, at any rate to the appearance of justice and sometimes to justice itself. Oddly enough this particular barrister instead of being an advocate on the Bench was unable to make up his mind. He became an extremely fair judge, but not a satisfactory one because he took so long to come to a decision. In his case a little more advocacy on the Bench might have been an advantage. Another very able,

fairminded judge died simply because he was temperament-
ally unsuited to the work.   He worried himself into the grave.

I think it is true to say that in almost every case where a
judge misbehaves in the sense that I have mentioned, his
intentions are good.   A judge who complains too soon about
the conduct of a solicitor has in mind the effect on that
solicitor's client and on the public, and his object is to prevent
such things from happening again.   He merely jumps too
quickly and does not give himself the opportunity of dis-
covering that the thing has not happened at all.   The very
rare cases where a judge's behaviour is wholly inexcusable and
not just ill-timed are where the remarks he makes are to satisfy
his own private whims or his own vanity and are not for the
benefit of the litigants before him or the community or the
legal profession.   Even the judge who said: " You are very
lucky in your jury " may well have wanted the man, of whose
guilt he had no doubt, to realise that he had not deceived the
judge, that he might not be so lucky with another jury in the
future and that he would be well advised to turn from his
criminal ways.

A prison chaplain asks why some judges tell prisoners that
they are beyond redemption—" a statement theologically
inaccurate and psychologically indefensible."   Very few
judges today indulge in this sort of pompous Victorian
nonsense.

It is only the less satisfactory judges who make undesirable
remarks when sentencing men.   Nothing should be added to
the actual sentence unless it is plainly in the interests of the
public, the accused or some other person connected with the
case.

When a judge in a civil or criminal case makes a scathing
attack on a party, witness or prisoner, he is usually abusing his

power but sometimes I doubt if he is aware of it. He has seen this kind of thing reported before or heard it done and thinks that it is up to him to continue the good work. I suspect that the judge who described a woman as worthless never considered whether he might be abusing his power.

There used to be a tendency among a very few judges to make jokes during a trial, not for the purpose of easing the tension, but in order to be able to listen to sycophantic laughter and perhaps to read their japes in the Press. I doubt if this happens today. It is quite a different thing to make the proceedings easier both for the litigants themselves and for counsel and solicitors appearing before the court. There is one judge today whose wit is as superb as his knowledge of the law is profound. It must be a great pleasure to appear before him, but he never condescends to a cheap jest: he merely makes the proceedings easier for everyone in his court.

But jests are not always out of place in court. Apart from easing tension they may have a proper object. For example, the late Mr. Justice Darling had a case in front of him where an unfortunate parson had been duped by a traveller in stocks and shares. (Peddling such commodities was then allowed.) The case was tried before a jury. Counsel for the pedlar urged that it was no part of the defendant's duty to decry his own wares. A man, he declared, has not got to cry " stinking fish." When Mr. Justice Darling came to sum up, he said this: " Counsel on behalf of the defendant has said to you, members of the jury, quite rightly, that the law of this country is *caveat emptor*, namely that the seller of goods has no duty to say that his goods are not worth buying. The buyer must look after himself. A fishmonger need not cry ' stinking fish.' This is very true, but, if a fishmonger knows that his fish do stink, he is not entitled to cry: ' Fresh fish, fresh fish,' nor is he any the more entitled to do this if he happens to know that his customer cannot smell.''

That was a perfectly fair way of putting the matter before the jury. Unfortunately that particular judge did not limit his wit to that sort of occasion.

And so it is with almost all judicial improprieties or mistakes in court. Except on the rarest occasions their object is a good one.

So much for unfair remarks during a trial. I shall suggest later in this lecture how they can be reduced, if not entirely eliminated. But I shall lead up to my suggestions by referring to what appears to be quite a different matter.

On April 2, 1970, *The Daily Telegraph* published an article by a barrister entitled '' When a judge makes a deal with counsel.'' In that article he said, among other things:

> '' Allegations have been made in several cases recently of secret deals between judges and lawyers about the sentence a prisoner will receive if he can be persuaded to plead guilty. Whatever their truth, such claims raise vital issues for those involved in the administration of justice.''

In a subsequent article in *The Daily Telegraph* of April 14, 1970, reference was made to the fact that a man may be induced to plead Guilty by the hope of a lesser sentence. Conversely, he may be frightened to plead Not Guilty for fear of a heavier one. It is as well that the public should fully understand the true position on both these matters.

I will deal with the second first.

Except in the case of the gravest crimes the fact that a man pleads Guilty is often a matter which can properly be taken into account when he comes to be sentenced. This will be particularly the case where a plea of Not Guilty would have involved a considerable ordeal for a witness, *e.g.* in a rape case. In other cases a long trial and great expense may be saved by a plea of Guilty. Moreover, apart from the saving of ordeals and costs, the fact that a man admits his guilt may enable the court, quite rightly, to take a more lenient view of his offence. The conduct of a first offender, for example, who admits his offence from the start and pleads Guilty, may justify the court in thinking that the man is really contrite and is unlikely to offend again. Whereas a first offender who puts up a false defence, suggests that everyone else is lying and commits perjury himself is not likely to give the judge much confidence in his plea, after conviction, that he is very sorry and won't do it again. As the second article in *The Daily Telegraph* points out, a man will not get an additional sentence for pleading Not Guilty and committing perjury, but, on the other hand, he will not get anything knocked off from what the judge considers to be a proper sentence.

It is the crime which carries the sentence, not the method of conducting the defence. The situation in civil cases is different. There aggravated damages are sometimes awarded by reason of the way in which a defence has been conducted, *e.g.* in a libel case. But not so in criminal cases. A judge would not be justified in adding on to the proper sentence for a rape an extra period because the defendant had raised a false defence of consent and put an obviously innocent girl through a horrible ordeal in the witness-box, but, on the other hand, if he expressed contrition from the start and pleaded Guilty, a justifiable sentence of seven years, for example, could be reduced to five.

But of course a problem still remains. If a man is told of these possibilities by his lawyer, as he certainly should be, is he going to plead Guilty when he is in fact not guilty? I cannot

conceive a sane man of good character doing this if he is
represented by a competent solicitor, except for some very
special reason, *e.g.* fear of publicity. It is, however, possible
that a man with previous convictions who happened to be
innocent on one occasion might be induced to plead Guilty
on that occasion. Being of low mentality and having been
disbelieved on the occasions when he was in fact telling lies,
he may think that he is likely to be disbelieved, although
telling the truth, and, being used to prison, he may conceivably be prepared to settle for a lesser sentence. He may
also, although innocent, be frightened of being cross-examined
owing to his previous experiences. It seems to me that this is
a possibility which cannot be avoided with the law as it is at
present, any more than you can prevent a person from committing suicide if he wants to do so. It is unfortunately these
low-grade, inadequate people who from time to time may
suffer injustice. If and when (as I suggest in my fourth lecture)
sentencing panels are introduced it might well be that such a
man's innocence would be discovered during the period when
his case was being carefully investigated by the panel, but I do
not see how such cases can otherwise be satisfactorily dealt
with.

I now come to the consideration of interviews between
judge and counsel. Most judges are prepared to see counsel
on both sides in a case, whether the case is a civil or a criminal
one. Sometimes the judge himself sends for counsel, more
usually counsel ask to see the judge. Private interviews
between counsel and the judge normally do no harm either to
the public or the parties, and they may do considerable good.
But this practice can be abused and I shall relate the worst
example of its abuse known to me when I have fully explained
the normal practice.

First let me take a typical case of my own. The health of one party was a relevant matter and a doctor was going to give evidence. I suspected that the person concerned was not aware of the nature of his illness. What I wanted to avoid was the party concerned suddenly being sent out of court whilst the doctor was giving evidence. In some cases that is worse than letting him hear the whole story. I someti nes found that inexperienced advocates do not know how to deal with such matters satisfactorily. So, when the time came, I said I was going to rise for a few minutes and I sent the usher to fetch counsel. I found out that my suspicions were correct. The plaintiff did not know what he was suffering from and the doctor did not want him to know. So I arranged with counsel some method by which all witnesses should be kept out of court during the doctor's evidence, so that the person concerned would not think that it was specially for his benefit.

That is a simple example. On other occasions counsel on both sides may want the guidance of the judge on some matter, for the purpose usually of saving costs or preventing somebody from being unnecessarily hurt in a matter. One counsel may say:

" My learned friend tells me that, if I call a certain witness, he is going to ask a particular question. Now it does not matter to my client's case in the least whether he asks the question or not but it does seem to me that such a question may do a serious injustice to the witness or to somebody else. We wondered if you, judge, could suggest some means by which my learned friend could get what he wants without such an injustice being caused."

Then, again, counsel may be trying to settle a case and the only issue between them is the amount of the damages. The less experienced counsel may be a little worried about agreeing to a particular sum in case it is too high or too low. They may both agree to go before the judge to see whether he will give them an opinion on the matter. Considerable costs can be saved in this way.

A topic on which I was more than once asked for guidance by counsel arose out of Legal Aid. Both counsel might be agreeable to settle an action on certain terms but they feared that in the result the only party who would benefit would be the Legal Aid Fund. Was there any proper method by which the plaintiff could get some benefit out of the litigation? I was rarely able to help in those particular cases because of the rules which then obtained but there was no harm in counsel asking.

In civil cases an interview with the judge and counsel may be particularly useful to enable them to arrive at a fair settlement satisfactory to both sides. It is perfectly true that the public is not present at those negotiations but neither is the public present when counsel or solicitors are discussing a case between themselves to arrive at a settlement. Hearings, except in rare cases, should always be in public but that does not mean to say that all the matters leading up to a hearing must be in public. It is in fact quite impossible that they should be.

In divorce cases an interview with the judge may be very useful because the parties wish to avoid any appearance of collusion. Moreover such interviews may very well ease matrimonial troubles. In the result I have never known of a civil case where an interview between the judge and counsel did any harm to either of the parties or to the public.

When one comes to criminal cases one is on more delicate ground because the public is a party to every criminal case. In every case, of course, civil or criminal, it is very wrong that any such interviews should take place unless all counsel involved in the matter are in front of the judge.

Lord Parker, the Lord Chief Justice, has said that both counsel should have access to the judge privately for proper reasons. It often happens that a man is charged with two or more offences, one less serious than the others. Counsel for the prosecution and the defence may come to the conclusion that from both their points of view a plea of Guilty to the lesser offence would be justifiable if the prosecution did not proceed on the more serious offence. In such a case the accused person must have admitted to his own counsel that he was guilty of the lesser offence or it would not be right for his counsel to allow him to plead Guilty. Counsel for the prosecution in such a case may, having regard to the evidence, think that there is a possibility that the accused may be acquitted of everything and that he certainly has a very good chance of being acquitted on the major charges. In the result counsel on both sides might agree that a proper result would be to have a plea of Guilty to the lesser charge and to drop the more serious one. They would then go before the judge, put the whole matter in front of him and ask if he agrees. If both counsel were experienced practitioners and known to the judge, most judges would normally agree to the course suggested being taken.

If all this were done in open court and the judge refused to agree, it might do the accused person considerable harm. Who could be sure that some information detrimental to him did not reach the jury?

In the sort of case to which I have last referred the question of sentence was not mentioned. But the most frequent occasion when counsel in a criminal case would like to consult the judge is on the matter of sentence. Jones may be prepared

to plead Guilty to a crime, provided he is not going to be sent
to prison, but otherwise he will fight to the last ditch. These
can be very difficult cases indeed, not least for counsel defending the accused. Let us assume that counsel for the prosecution approaches counsel for the defence in such a case and says
that he is prepared to withdraw the more serious charges if the
accused will plead Guilty to the least serious charge, and further,
that he is prepared to go before the judge and ask him whether
he will send the accused to prison if in fact he pleads Guilty
only to the least serious charge. Counsel for the defence
would be under a duty to report the conversation to his client.
" All right," says his client, " if you promise me that I shan't
be sent to prison I will plead Guilty to the third charge. But
I am not guilty, mind you." What does counsel for the
defence do? Obviously he might be able to go through the
motions of forcing his client to use the words " all right, I
am guilty," it being obvious both to counsel and the client
that he was only saying the words under compulsion. Plainly
that would be wrong. If the accused says to his counsel:
" Go ahead, I want you to do this and I am quite prepared to
plead Guilty in court but I repeat to you that I am not guilty,"
should counsel agree to the suggestion or say that in those circumstances his client must either maintain his plea of Not
Guilty and go ahead with the trial or instruct other solicitors
and counsel?

I think he should take the latter course, but that is not really
a matter with which these lectures are concerned. I am concerned with the position of the judge. Whatever, then, may
have taken place between counsel and his client, the parties go
before the judge and ask him whether, in the circumstances
of the case, he would be prepared, in effect, to give an under-
taking not to send the man to prison.

Lord Parker said in the Court of Appeal on April 24, 1970 (*R.* v. *Turner, The Times* April 25, 1970), that a judge should never say what sentence he would impose if the accused pleads Guilty, lest the man might assume from this that he might fare worse if he pleaded Not Guilty. On that occasion Lord Parker made the following observations:

(1) Counsel could properly advise his client that a Guilty plea might enable the court to give a lesser sentence.

(2) The accused, having considered that advice, must have complete freedom of choice to plead Guilty or Not Guilty.

(3) There must be freedom of access between counsel and judge but both counsel must be present and the solicitor for the accused if he wishes. As far as possible justice should be administered in open court and interviews with the judge should only be sought when really necessary.

(4) The judge should only mention sentence if he is able to say that the sentence would be the same whatever the plea of the accused.

All judges will now normally follow the view expressed by the Court of Appeal. But there can be exceptions to nearly every rule and most judges would feel at liberty to depart from the rule in quite exceptional circumstances, *e.g.* where to comply with it might cause distress or hardship.

Judges do not always agree to suggestions forwarded by both counsel at these private interviews. Many years ago a man was charged with murder. Counsel for the prosecution realised that in the circumstances of the case the jury might acquit him both of murder and of manslaughter and, when counsel for the defence offered to plead Guilty to manslaughter, he was quite prepared to advise the Director of Public Prosecutions to accept this plea. So they went before the judge, who refused to agree to it. In the end the jury acquitted the man of both murder and manslaughter. The man's defence was that he was carrying a firearm for the purpose of committing suicide and not for the purpose of hurting the dead man. He accordingly pleaded Guilty to a further charge that was made against him of carrying firearms with intent to endanger life, *i.e.* his own. The judge was so angry at his having been acquitted of both murder and manslaughter, when he could have given him ten years on a plea of Guilty to manslaughter, that he gave him the maximum sentence of one year's imprisonment with hard labour for an offence which was less than that of attempted suicide (a crime in those days). This judge had a reputation (not altogether deserved) for being judicial on the Bench. He was not judicial on that occasion.

In the case in which Lord Parker made the observations mentioned the court was mainly concerned with the position of the accused. But the public also has to be considered. It seems to me that the only harm such interviews between counsel and the judge and such arrangements can do is if the public become suspicious that there is something underhand going on. I therefore agree with the writer of the article in *The Daily Telegraph* that it would be a good thing if, when such arrangements have been made, the judge informs the public in open court roughly what has happened. It seems to me that, if that expedient is adopted, in the normal case there is no reason whatever for discontinuing the present practice.

The writer of the article also suggests that there should be rules laid down for such arrangements. There, with respect, I disagree. Such matters, I have no doubt, are best left to the good sense and integrity of the judge and counsel appearing in front of him. There are so many permutations and combinations that it is impossible to provide for each case. It is much better that no definite rules should be made on the subject, other than the general rules enunciated by Lord Parker. There will of course be exceptional cases where it is undesirable to make more than a brief statement in court. One of them is mentioned in the article in question, *i.e.* where the accused may be suffering from cancer yet unaware of the fact. Normally, however, a statement should serve to dispel any suspicions by the public.

If it is true, as suggested in the article, that there have been occasions when the judge has initiated talks with counsel with a view to a prisoner pleading Guilty, not so much because of his regard for the result of a particular case, but in order to lighten his heavy list, that was very wrong indeed. Plainly no judge should initiate a promise to a man in order to persuade him to change his plea of Not Guilty to Guilty, least of all for the purpose of lightening the judge's list. On the other hand, as Lord Parker said, it is perfectly proper for counsel, who is satisfied of his client's guilt, to suggest to him that he would be well advised to plead Guilty.

This leads me to the case with which I was concerned. Even in this case it is right to say that, improper as was the behaviour of four judges, one of their primary objects was the attainment of justice. But I fear that in the case of three of the judges there was also a secondary object which was unworthy of them. I am quite sure that this case would not have occurred today, but I think it is desirable that it should be recorded. There are several lessons which can be learned from it, and, unless those lessons are learned, it could happen again and this could properly give rise to far worse comment than was made in the article in *The Daily Telegraph*.

Two men (I will call them Smith and Robinson) were charged at the Old Bailey with obtaining goods by false pretences. It was alleged that they had formed a fraudulent company for the purpose of obtaining goods on credit and selling them for cash without any intention of paying the creditors. This is what lawyers call a long-firm fraud. I appeared for Smith and another counsel for Robinson. Robinson was a young man with no previous convictions and he had made a statement to the police which, if true, showed that both he and my client were guilty. My client was a much older man and had several previous convictions for similar offences. There was, however, extremely little evidence against him and the statement made to the police by Robinson could not be used in evidence to show that my client was guilty. On the other hand, if Robinson pleaded Guilty, he could be called as a witness for the prosecution and he could then give evidence against my client.

In fact, however, Robinson refused to plead Guilty and the case accordingly started against both the defendants. At lunch-time the prosecution had concluded its case and the judge said to counsel for the prosecution: " After lunch I shall want to know what evidence you say there is against Smith." The court then adjourned for lunch. For some reason, which I do not now remember, I felt morally certain that the judge had asked to see counsel for Robinson. So, before the court reassembled, I spoke to Robinson's counsel and I told him that I did not want him to answer the question I was going to ask if he did not want to do so but, if he did answer it, I should use his answer in my speech to the jury. I then inquired whether the judge had asked to see him during the adjournment and he said that he was not prepared to answer. It was obvious to me from this that he had in fact been to see the judge. There could only be one reason for this. The judge wanted to persuade counsel to get his client, Robinson, to plead Guilty so that he should be available as a witness for the prosecution against Smith.

We went back into court. What happened then was this. Without a word being spoken, counsel for Robinson nodded to the clerk of the court and the clerk then addressed Robinson as follows: " Robinson, I understand that you wish to change your plea from Not Guilty to Guilty. Is that so? " Robinson said: " Yes, it is." He then formally pleaded Guilty and became available as a witness for the prosecution.

He duly gave evidence which, if true, completely damned my client. When I came to cross-examine him I asked him why he had changed his plea. He gave no reason. I then asked him this: " Have you not been promised by the judge through your counsel that, if you changed your plea and gave evidence against my client, you would not be sent to prison? " Robinson said: " No." I looked at the judge and waited for him to intervene, but he did nothing. The case then proceeded and eventually my client was called and gave his evidence. He denied his guilt but he was not a very good witness and, after the summing-up and a short retirement, the jury found him guilty.

When the judge asked me if I had anything to say about sentence I said this: " My Lord, in view of the fact that there is likely to be an appeal in this case, I feel bound to ask you, did you not in fact promise my learned friend that, if his client changed his plea to Guilty and gave evidence for the prosecution, you would not send him to prison? " The judge replied: " I am not bound to answer that question." I said: " Of course your lordship is not bound to answer it, but I felt bound to ask it." The judge then sentenced my client to eighteen months' imprisonment without hard labour, a very lenient sentence indeed and I cannot think of any reason for the judge imposing it except in the hope that my client would be so pleased that he would refuse to appeal.

After my client had been sentenced, the judge was in a slight quandary and he endeavoured to get out of it by postponing sentence on Robinson till the next session. This meant that the unfortunate young man had to spend a month or at least two or three weeks in prison. He was obviously furious but he did not say anything.

My client then appealed against his conviction. I approached Robinson's counsel and asked him to confirm that the judge had promised him that, if his client pleaded Guilty and gave evidence for the prosecution, he would not send him to prison and he told me that this promise had in fact been made. So an appeal was accordingly launched upon these grounds and upon the further ground that the judge knew that Robinson had told a lie in cross-examination when he said that that promise had not been made and that the judge had failed to tell the jury. The judge who examined applications for leave to appeal (du Parcq J., as he then was) gave leave but unfortunately was not on the appeal court.

Normally, when counsel can give information to a court about what has happened during a case, he gives that information from his place at the Bar without taking the oath but, in case of accidents, I had also asked the court for leave to call counsel for Robinson as a witness, so that he could give in evidence what had actually taken place between him and the judge. The court (presided over by the Lord Chief Justice already mentioned) refused to hear counsel from the Bar and refused to let me call him to give evidence and, when they gave judgment, they said that it was quite plain that nothing of the kind suggested by me in my Notice of Appeal had happened but that all that had taken place was that counsel for Robinson had very wisely advised his client to change his plea to Guilty. This was simply untrue, but the Court of Criminal Appeal refused to allow evidence of the truth of the matter to be given.

One rather odd feature about the case was the failure of the Press to mention it at all. There was no sensational news at the time of my case and why it was not reported I do not know to this day.

I said that the primary object of all these judges was the attainment of justice and so it was. They all firmly believed that my client was a guilty man and that he should not be allowed to escape just because there wasn't enough evidence against him, or just because the judge in the court below had behaved improperly. But unquestionably a secondary object of the judges in the Court of Criminal Appeal was to prevent the conduct of the judge in the court below from being made public. In order to achieve this secondary object, they said something in their judgment which was untrue. I said earlier that this would not have happened today, but it could happen again, if more precautions are not taken before a judge is appointed.

I suggest that no one should be appointed to a judgeship or magistracy until he has shown that he is fit for the appointment. In a good many cases he has been a recorder before his appointment but this will not, in my view, show sufficiently whether he is fit for a permanent judgeship. Except in the case of the Recorders of London, Liverpool and Manchester, which are full-time judgeships, a recorder is a judge four times a year for a few days. As I mentioned earlier, one day Mr. A will be recorder and Mr. B will be appearing in front of him. Shortly afterwards the position may be reversed. It is therefore unlikely that many recorders will throw their weight about during their very temporary sittings on the Bench.

The judge referred to on page 59, who was far too slow and undecided to be satisfactory on the Bench, had been a recorder for six years. Either he cannot have shown himself in his true colours while acting as recorder or, alternatively, no attempts were made to observe his performances in that capacity.

No one should be appointed as a High Court or county court judge or stipendiary magistrate if he is likely to " throw his weight about." Such a man may be an excellent lawyer and have an excellent intellect and, if of exceptional calibre, might possibly be appointed direct to the Court of Appeal, but he will do immense harm as a judge of first instance or a magistrate. You cannot expect the average judge to be modest at heart. Success at the Bar normally requires at least a modicum of conceit and he cannot drop it on appointment. But he should be able to control the look of the thing. Those who cannot should not be appointed. Good manners among judges of first instance are as important as a good legal brain, even more important in the case of the lesser judges. Indeed, good manners are very important in life. They make good motorists as well as good judges.

A barrister who is under consideration for a judgeship should have to undergo a probationary period before he is finally appointed. This can be done by making him a Commissioner of Assize, if necessary several times, or a deputy county court judge or a deputy magistrate. Or, if the Beeching Report is implemented, he can become one of the new part-time recorders. And steps should be taken to observe and inquire into his behaviour. They do this in at least one

European country. The probationary period should be longer rather than shorter.

I think that the advantage of judges being appointed from the Bar is very great. Having been advocates themselves, they know what is happening much better than someone who has been brought up in a judicial profession, as happens elsewhere in Europe. But the one disadvantage is the possibility that such a person may be wholly unsuited for the position.

An engaged couple who stay in the house of the parents of one of them can behave themselves well during a single week-end. They should, therefore, stay for a fortnight or so. You are bound to behave naturally with your own parents over a prolonged period, even though someone else is present. So a barrister sitting on the Bench for the first time might behave himself for a short time but, if he were likely to make an unsatisfactory judge, he would probably disclose the fact if he sat for three or four weeks. Indeed some would-be judges sitting as deputy-judges show by their treatment of the usher or the parking-place attendant that they are not suitable for appointment.

In no circumstances should the Lord Chief Justice be appointed except from among the judges. The position is obviously an extremely important one and it is vital that before his appointment the Lord Chief Justice should be known to be a judge of great ability and good manners. It was the then Lord Chief Justice who was mainly responsible for the behaviour of the Court of Criminal Appeal in the case to which I have just referred and in another case to which I refer later (pp. 149–150) and he had not even been a recorder before his appointment as Lord Chief Justice. His main virtue as a judge was his command of simple English, which was quite superb. But he was by common consent the worst Lord

Chief Justice we have had this century and probably for much longer than that.

There are objections to the probationary system and I will refer to them. It would be necessary for possible High Court judges to go as Commissioners of Assize for a period of at least three or four weeks, probably more. If subsequently they were not appointed to the Bench, it would become known that they had been passed over. It can be said that it is one thing simply to be passed over and another to be passed over after trial. Undoubtedly it would be unfortunate for those wanting judicial preferment if they went as Commissioners and were never appointed. On the other hand, this happens with the present system. More than one barrister has been appointed Commissioner and not thereafter been made a judge.

It could also be said that there would be special difficulties in regard to the Chancery Division where the judges never now go on circuit. There was an occasion when they were sent on circuit but the result in criminal cases was so appalling that it was never tried again. Coming from the rarefied atmosphere of the Chancery Division, they were horrified at what they heard and their sentences were astronomic. There seems to be no good reason, however, why members of the Chancery Bar should not go on circuit for the trial of civil cases only. On the whole, the Chancery lawyer is better able to adapt his mind to matters of common law than vice versa.

It can further be said that the natural climax of the successful barrister's career is appointment to the Bench and that in that way only can he achieve security. Before the war successful members of the Bar could save up quite enough to provide for their old age and retirement, but since the war this is only possible to a very limited degree owing to the extent of taxation. Most other professional men either have a pension or something which they can sell, *e.g.* their share in a solicitor's practice. The barrister, unless appointed to the Bench, is dependent entirely upon his own savings.

The answer to this argument is, I think, that everyone who is called to the Bar knows of this disadvantage before he enters the profession and, secondly, that it cannot be right in the public interest to appoint someone who is not fitted to be a judge just in order to provide for his old age. Even if this probationary system is adopted, there will still be occasional unsatisfactory appointments, but they should be very, very few. With the present system there are not many, but there are too many. As a county court judge I must have tried twenty or thirty thousand cases. Think of the harm I must have done if I was not suitable for the appointment. I do not say that I was suitable and I may have done harm, but it is too late to worry about that. Indeed, the more harm I did, the more occasion there is to take steps to prevent other bad judges from being appointed.

I ought to make it plain that of course the Lord Chancellor is careful in his present appointments and, as I have already said, he consults his own well-informed department and distinguished members of the legal profession before making such appointments. All I am saying is that there should be an obligatory trial period and that even more care should be taken to ensure the suitability of the candidate. I have heard or read of complaints against certain individual judges in the last thirty years. Few, if any, of them would have been appointed if the suggested additional care had been taken. Let me also make it plain that I am not now referring to the " sieving " process. That is necessary to preserve the integrity of the Bench, and all the unsatisfactory judges to whom I have referred were persons of the highest integrity.

Another suggestion which, had it been adopted before I
was appointed, would certainly have made me a better judge,
is that each judge on appointment should be warned by a
senior judge of the dangers of abuse of power and particularly
against:

   (1) Making unfair remarks.
   (2) Summing up for a conviction.
   (3) Not appreciating the fact that the average witness is a
        stranger to the court and needs help.

I think that a good many judges (and for a time I was
certainly one of them) do not appreciate the difficulties of
giving evidence. Because few witnesses ask for a glass of
water and fewer still faint, that does not mean that many of
them are not extremely frightened. Most of them put an
extraordinarily good face on it and this is one of the reasons
why their difficulties are not fully appreciated. Lawyers are
so used to seeing witnesses go in and out of the witness-box,
taking the oath on the way (I shall have something to say
about the oath later), that we do not realise that their hearts
may be beating twice as fast as usual and their heads going
round in a whirl. It is difficult enough for some people to
tell a story accurately to their friends in the most congenial
circumstances. How can they be expected to do it when they
go into court for the first time, with the judge and counsel
wigged and robed and the fear of being sent to prison if they
so much as cough out of turn?

One law student made an interesting suggestion. He said
that on appointment judges should be sent to school and
should receive some degree of training. It is absurd, he argued,
that he may one day be a specialist silk and the next day an
omniscient judge who is expected to cope with every sort of
problem. He also pointed out that few, if any, judges have

taken degrees in social science and he suggested that judges should start with a sabbatical year in which they should travel and visit universities and participate in seminars and discussions with both lawyers and social scientists and should also travel abroad to get first-hand experience of other systems in action. He went on: " This is not to suggest that I wholly denigrate the quality and excellence of our judiciary, but it is also dangerous to adopt the assumption that, because an institution is very good or even one of the best there is, it could not be rendered even better." He added that there should be some sort of organised instruction mounted by experienced judges who in particular should be specialists in the field pertaining to the region or division in which the new judge is ultimately going to sit.

I think that there is a good deal in this suggestion, though a year is perhaps too long. Continuity is important. During the period of schooling the judge would be divorced from active practice either at the Bar or on the Bench. But in a period of three to six months the judge could learn a lot. At the least he could attend lectures and discussions on sociological and psychological problems and he could visit prisons. I would still give high priority to a lesson from an experienced judge on the treatment of witnesses, advocates and prisoners.

A prison chaplain presents a careful, reasoned argument for more discussions between judges and other people concerned with the social situation.

" How on earth do judges manage the problem of sentencing?" he asks. " From my experience," he answers, " they largely rely on a combination of 90 per cent. inspiration and 10 per cent. desperation. This is not wholly the fault of the lawyers. They did not compile the syllabus of professional examinations so as to exclude criminology altogether. Nor is there any place where they can regularly meet prison officers and probation officers and others and discuss the kind of sentence thought to be effective for a particular kind of offender."

I think that there is a great deal in what this chaplain says, but personally, for the reasons I give later, I do not think judges ought to sentence offenders for serious crimes at all. I think this should be done by a special panel. I deal with this matter in detail in the fourth of these lectures. The chaplain goes on:

" We rightly respect our judiciary, but we have made the mistake in the past of placing them on a pedestal and of regarding them too much as symbols of semi-divine wisdom and justice."

He also criticises the judges for not consulting the police before devising the judges' rules.[1] The whole area of the judges' rules and questioning and detention by the police requires overhauling. At the moment people are regularly being detained illegally for questioning but, if the police did not act in this way, they would only bring a very much smaller percentage of criminals to justice. Moreover the judges' rules hamper the police from making perfectly reasonable inquiries in order to find out who has committed a crime.

A section of the public, including some distinguished lawyers, tends to favour the suspected criminal. I have never yet understood why a man, who is thought to have committed a crime, should not be asked questions about that crime and why his refusal to answer questions should not be given in evidence against him, provided in each case that no

---

[1] Rules laid down by the judges as a guide to the police when dealing with suspects.

improper pressure is brought to bear upon him. Why should a man not be asked to incriminate himself, provided he is not bullied into answering?

A suggestion which would do away with the need for the police acting illegally is that any police officer who had reasonable grounds for thinking that a person might be able to give information about a crime should be entitled, at any time of the day or night, to convey that person before a justice of the peace, before whom the person conveyed should be required to answer any questions, even though incriminating. There should be a panel of justices who would be available to hear such examinations and a panel of solicitors who would be available to represent the accused. If the accused refused to answer questions, his refusal could be given in evidence at his trial if he were subsequently prosecuted. Everything said by the accused before the justice, including any admissions, should be admissible at his trial, but no other statements of the accused should be admissible, unless they took place as part of or during the commission of the crime or during a " hue and cry." The solicitor present for the benefit of the accused should only be there in order to see that there is no improper pressure brought to bear on the accused. He should not be entitled to advise the accused, for example, not to answer any questions.

If this suggestion does not commend itself to Parliament, at any rate something should be done. Although occasionally at the moment a judge comments on the fact that a person has been detained quite illegally at a police station, for the most part the illegal practice of the police is winked at. I am not criticising the police for indulging in it. If they did not, they would not be able to discharge their duties half so efficiently. But I do criticise the legal profession, the public and Parliament for allowing the practice to continue. Steps should be taken to give the police satisfactory powers to enable them to detect crime without themselves breaking the law.

A difficult and important matter with which a judge is sometimes concerned is the effect on other people of the result of a case. In a criminal trial a judge has a duty to the man being tried and to the public and he may have a third duty, namely, to a vital witness in the case. People are apt to forget that not only the relatives of the accused are affected by the verdict and sentence, but that there may be a witness or witnesses who are very seriously affected too. Police officers may often be seriously affected by a verdict of acquittal where the acquittal can only have been on the ground that the jury at least thought it possible that police officers had behaved in a grossly improper manner.

In rape cases, where the defence has been consent, an acquittal may seriously tarnish a woman's character. Indeed on one occasion a girl committed suicide after such an acquittal. In fact it seems to me that this is one of the most difficult matters with which a judge has to deal. If a man is acquitted of rape and his defence has been that of consent, a judge must not impugn the verdict of the jury, but at the same time he may want to say something comforting to the woman concerned. It cannot be at all an easy thing to do. It is perfectly true that the verdict of the jury merely shows that they were not satisfied beyond all reasonable doubt of the man's guilt. It does not show that they disbelieved the woman; they merely thought the man's story possible, and therefore they had to acquit him. But it cannot be at all easy to point this out to the woman concerned without at the same time appearing to be suggesting that the prisoner may really have been guilty. And that is true. He may have been guilty, but his guilt was not sufficiently proved. In the result grave injustice may have been done to the chief witness for the prosecution, but how this is to be completely avoided I do not know, though possibly the services of a welfare officer might help.

Then sometimes a person who is not a party to the proceedings and is not a witness is criticised by the judge. Normally a judge would not make adverse criticisms of a person or company without giving them the opportunity to appear and to give an explanation of their conduct, but there must be cases where this is virtually impossible or undesirable, for example where the question at issue is which of two innocent parties is to suffer because of the misbehaviour of a third party who has disappeared or, even if he has not disappeared, where both parties are throwing the blame upon him and neither of them wishes to call him as a witness. A judge's first consideration must be a fair trial of the action before him. If both parties are laying the blame upon somebody else whom neither party wishes to call, the judge cannot possibly give that third person the opportunity of making a statement in court. Possibly in a very rare type of case he might give leave to that person to make a statement in court after the case had been decided.

On September 11, 1969, a letter was written to *The Times* by the head of one of the television companies complaining that his company had been censured by a Divisional Court without having the opportunity to reply to such censure. The writer complained that this showed there was a defect in the law. He said that the English system was reputed to be the finest in the world and was noted for its fairness, but, he added, perhaps it has one flaw: " A judge can pass comments freely, sometimes too freely, about parties who are not permitted to be in court and who are therefore denied any right of reply." This is not entirely accurate as, unless a case is being heard *in camera*, everyone can be in court, but it is true to say that occasionally a judge does pass comments too freely about a party who is not in fact in court and that a person who is in court may not be given the chance to reply.

Normally, however, a judge will give the person about whom he proposes to comment or has commented an opportunity of giving an explanation if he wants it. This is only fair and, if every judge upon his appointment were given advice by a senior judge, complaints of unfairness would in all probability be very much reduced.

No judge is perfect and every judge is bound to make a mistake in one direction or another, though I am sure that there are many judges who have never criticised a person unfairly and never will. It would be quite impossible to prevent the occasional lapse by legislation. The remedy is more care in the appointment of judges and good advice to each new judge. Moreover it would have been open to the writer of the letter to ask for leave to make a statement in court. But some people could not afford this expense.

CHAPTER 3

VIRTUES AND VICES

Another schoolboy's comments considered at length—"judicial
ignorance"—contempt of court—the Welsh case—some judges' lack
of imagination—why does a witness have to be old, ill or pregnant
to get a seat?—why 2,000 people went to prison each year by mistake
—putting witnesses at ease—the oath—remoteness of some judges—
judges' private lives—problem of the motor-car—judges' holidays—
judges' care to avoid appearance of favouritism—trial of accident
cases—national insurance instead?—injustice due to lack of imagination.

ONE of the comments which I had from a schoolboy makes so
many points of interest that I think it worth repeating almost
in full. I shall intersperse it with my own comments.

"The image of the judge in modern society is an anach-
ronism. It has changed little if at all. They tend to
come from a small conservative section of the community,
very much upper class, major public schools, almost
exclusively Oxford and Cambridge."

My analysis of the schools and universities from which
judges come shows that this young man is to some extent
correct, as far as schools and universities are concerned.

He goes on: "They are often the sons of judges or of
knights or of generals or of landed gentry."

He is not so accurate there. Of the 117 judges and magistrates only a very, very few were the sons of judges or knights
or generals but I must concede that eleven of them married
the daughters of serving officers. Serving officers led the field
by a long way as fathers-in-law of judges. Parsons were a
poor second (4), judges almost last (2).

Without investigating the assets of the parents of each of the judges mentioned I cannot say for certain that they are not the sons of landed gentry, but, judging from their addresses and my knowledge of many of them, I shall be surprised if more than a small number of the parents of modern judges came from the class which may properly be described as " landed gentry."

The young man goes on: " They seem at odds with the modern welfare state ideals."

I do not know where he gets this from. If there are any judges today who do not approve of the welfare state, there must be very few of them. But the statement is so important that I must deal with it, particularly as it derives some support from something said by Professor MacGibbon, the Dean of the Faculty of Law at Edinburgh University. He said in a lecture:

> " What can elderly judges know about the way people live, particularly young people or poor people? They do tend, I suggest, to be not entirely in the picture. They are old, they tend not to sympathise with wild views, and they tend not to understand the problems of poverty, and indeed some of the problems of social justice. I think this is an inherent defect in every country's courts."

Professor MacGibbon's remarks may apply to Scotland, but I am not sufficiently informed on the matter. I am surprised, however, that a professor of Edinburgh University should talk about " elderly judges . . . in every country," when in England at any rate the average age on appointment is 53 and the average age of all judges sitting today is 60.

I should not have expected the schoolboy to have had much experience of English county courts, but I should be interested to know how many English county courts Professor MacGibbon had visited before passing his strictures. And is he not aware of the county court judge who over a hundred years ago said to a man in the course of a case: " You are a harpy, preying on the vitals of the poor "? (It was a famous case, as the judge was sued for slander—unsuccessfully. *Scott* v. *Stansfield* (1868) L.R. 3 Ex. 220.) I am not saying that the Professor might not have given better judgments on points of law than some county court judges, but, when he says that they tend not to understand the problems of poverty or social justice, he shows that he is insufficiently acquainted—if indeed he is acquainted at all—with the way in which English county court judges do their work. He might have been better advised to criticise judges for making unfair remarks, as occasionally they do, in common with Professor MacGibbon.

I was interested to see that " The Londoner " in the London *Evening News* of September 28, 1969, took up the Professor's statement. Among other things he said:

" I have noted again and again outstanding examples of compassion, understanding and kindness shown by our judiciary, examples which in the nature of things would be less likely to be shown by the young and immature. . . . On the whole it is best that those who have known a fair amount of life's encounter should adjudicate when we squabble or go off the rails."

But I must return to the young man:

" Judges," he says, " more than members of any other profession seem removed from ordinary everyday life. In wig and majesty they spend most of their working days aloof from their fellow men. Their private lives away from the Inns of Court seem to be confined to their clubs, *e.g.* the Reform, the Garrick or the Oxford and Cambridge."

This young man has obviously read and relied on Anthony Sampson's entertaining *Anatomy of Britain*. I can only say that, as far as I was concerned, though I admit to being a member of the Garrick, my private life was like that of many of my friends who are not lawyers and so to my knowledge is the private life of many other judges.

The young man goes on: " The assize judge who travels in his own car doesn't even stay at hotels as other mortals do, but in special lodgings."

If the assize judge does not travel in his own car he will travel in a specially reserved compartment in the train. The reason for this is that it would be highly undesirable for the judge who is presiding at the local assizes to come into outside contact with witnesses, counsel, solicitors, parties and conceivably jurors. This he might well do if he stayed at an hotel or travelled with members of the public. (Although counsel visit judges at their lodgings, a judge would not invite counsel engaged on a case in front of him without asking his opponent at the same time.)

One of my complaints about the way in which divorce was handled between the year of my appointment in 1949 and the 1960s was that the main object seemed to be to get through as many divorces as possible. Almost any room would serve as a court. One result of this was that some county court judges had to share the same lavatory as the litigants and witnesses. Many people who have seen a judge in court do not recognise him without his wig. It is highly undesirable, in my view, that the judge standing next to a man in the lavatory should have the opportunity of hearing himself described as a " cock-eyed old so-and-so " or, worse still, being told something about the case which he is trying. I agree that it may be good for a judge to hear unfavourable comments about himself but, while trying cases, judges should be segregated from the parties and witnesses.

The comments, again inspired by Mr. Sampson, proceed:

" British judges have continued in their detachment from modern social developments and from society much more than their American and continental counterparts. They are sceptical of the new sciences, psychology and sociology and some (*e.g.* Mr. Justice Darling) even prided themselves upon their ignorance of everyday life."

There are certainly a few judges today who have spoken slightingly of psychiatrists and it may be also of sociologists. What was good enough for their fathers is good enough for them. There are very few of such judges and they are dying out. In this age of new techniques, the modern judge is prepared to consider new aids for arriving at a decision and, in criminal cases, new considerations about punishment. Most of them are far more broad-minded than their predecessors. The people who have written to me saying in effect that there is no such thing as a " modern " judge, because, they say, all judges are conservative and do not move with the times, cannot have had any substantial experience of today's courts.

Feigned judicial ignorance is so often commented on that I ought to deal with it fully. It is thought by some that there is a tradition whereby a judge is not to be expected to be in touch with current affairs, particularly current expressions of speech. The President of the Legal Society of one of the larger universities writes:

" Reading the Law Reports of the 19th century I feel sure that many judges might have said as did Gwendolen in the *Importance of Being Earnest*: ' I am glad to say that I have never seen a spade.' "

But if there ever was such a tradition, it no longer exists.

Every judge is today reasonably well in touch with ordinary current affairs and ordinary current expressions. Naturally the extent of knowledge of each judge will vary according to his tastes. One of the judges whose hobby is the Turf will fully understand the expression " tens bar," [1] but I should be surprised if many of my listeners or readers who did not go in for racing would have the faintest idea what it meant. If you do not know what is meant by " tens bar," why should I be expected to know who is top of the charts? Indeed a judge who is unacquainted with " pop " groups may have to ask the names of the young people who make up the Beatles if it is relevant to the case which he is trying.

Again, while there are plenty of colloquial and modern expressions which I know, there are no doubt many that I don't, and, when a judge is trying a case, he must not pretend to know something which he doesn't in fact know. The origin of this behaviour on the part of judges, which many people think is just an attempt to be funny, is that, while judges are presumed to know all matters of general and certain knowledge, *e.g.* that England is an island and that the day of the week is Thursday, strictly speaking everything else has to be proved in front of them. No doubt there were sometimes judges who sought to gain a cheap laugh by asking a question of which they already knew the answer but which they considered could be legally justified by the rule to which I have referred. But that is a thing of the past. And, if you have a hobby which is not shared by the judge, don't be too contemptuous of him. He may have several hobbies which you don't share. In any event, when he asks a question, he really wants to know the answer and he is not feigning ignorance.

[1] This expression is sometimes used by a bookmaker when shouting the odds. It means " I will offer 10 to 1 or more against any horse in the race except the favourite."

" Where, then," asks the young man, " does the modern judge differ at all from the judges of Victorian days or even such characters as Jeffreys? In my opinion the difference lies in the curtailment of the power they wield rather than their personal image. Since that first document on human rights, Magna Carta, British judges were the law-makers. Common law based on precedent and the law of equity based on judges, with common sense and fair play, were the mainstay of the judiciary. The modern judge, on the other hand, is becoming more and more an administrator of the statutory laws laid down by Parliament. This is the logical outcome of the ever-increasing perplexities of modern specialisation. No one judge could know all the complex tax laws, every new company law, criminal laws, etc. Another change is that since 1959 the obligatory retirement age of the judge is 75. Yet for all their wigs and pomp and dusty old-fashioned splendour the British judge in modern society, where every man and every thing is supposed to have his and its price, has one supreme advantage over all his foreign peers. He is unbribable. He does not owe allegiance to any one political party and, due to the fact that once he is appointed he is irremovable until his seventy-fifth birthday, he can judge impartially without worrying about keeping his position or political implications. So, in conclusion, the current image of the modern judge is not yet as up to date as one might wish it to be, but he seems to be moving in the right direction after hundreds of years of being static."

I doubt if anyone will disagree with me if I say that, however judges come out of my researches, schoolboys come out very well.

I propose now to deal with contempt of court.

It should never be necessary for a judge to abuse his power. He is in such a strong position. He can fine or send to prison anyone who misbehaves (this does not apply to a magistrate but he has at any rate plenty of policemen to help him to keep order in his court). In fact people in court behave themselves extremely well. It was an isolated occurrence when a man threw tomatoes at the Court of Appeal. And he missed. I have only once exacted a penalty from someone for contempt of court. I will tell you the circumstances so that you can decide whether I abused my power or not.

I was trying a case between a landlord and a tenant. The landlord was seeking to turn out the tenant, who was an old woman, on the ground of nuisance or annoyance. Unfortunately the old lady had reached an age, possibly prematurely, when she was unable to control herself and she abused and assaulted people all round her. The landlord was represented by solicitors and counsel. The old lady represented herself. The whole street, it seemed, came to see the old lady turned out and they sat in serried ranks at the back of the court. When it became her turn to say something, there was, after a short time, a moan or sound of derision from the back of the court and the usher silenced it. When this happened a third time I said: " There must be no further noise from the back of the court. If there is, I shall deal with the offender for contempt of court." For some minutes after that there was silence. Then the old lady said something and there was a solitary sound of derision from the back of the court. I said: " Who did that? " and the old lady, pointing a finger at a man, said: " It was him." A man got up and said: " I only coughed." If he had denied doing anything I couldn't have decided the matter against him because I would only have had his word and the old lady's word and I had not observed myself who had done it. But it was certainly not a cough. So I said: " Let that man come forward." He came to the front of the court, and I said to him: " You are fined half-a-crown for contempt of court." He said: " I have only got two shillings." I said: " All right, we'll take that."

The disturbances in the High Court early this year when some young Welshmen misbehaved in open court gave rise to some discussion. Some people queried how the judge, who was the person insulted, could be a judge in his own cause. The answer to that question is that the judge was not insulted in his own personal capacity but as the Queen's justice. It was an insult to the court rather than the man. Moreover, as everyone in court could (subject to one qualification) see what happened, there could be no doubt in anyone's mind that a contempt had been committed.

The qualification is that in the particular circumstances of that case it might have been claimed by one or more offenders that they took no part in the misbehaviour, did not know that it was going to occur and simply came into court out of curiosity. Had there been serious disputes of fact the judge would have been a witness. As a witness he would be capable of making a mistake. Was it A who did such-and-such or B? The judge could have mistaken one for the other. Could he then have adjudicated? Could he have said: " The accused denies that he did it, but I prefer my own evidence on that matter. I have known myself for many years as a most reliable witness."

The accused's evidence would have been given on oath and would have been subject to cross-examination. Not so the judge's. Indeed the judge would not have given evidence at all. Contempt of court is a criminal charge and it seems to

me that, should a case arise where there is a real dispute as to
what happened in front of the judge, there would have to be a
trial before another judge and the first judge would have to
give evidence like any other witness.

I might have been involved in such a case myself. I was
driving to court one day via some small streets and, when I was
three or four hundred yards away from the court, I was held
up by a stationary parked car on one side of the road and a
coalman delivering coal on the other. If the coalman had
moved his lorry a foot, I could have got through. So I stopped
and went up to him and asked him if he would be kind enough
to move his lorry. He said that he would do so when he had
finished delivering the coal. I said to him: " I would be
terribly grateful if you would do it at once." He said: " You
will have to wait." I said: " As a matter of fact I am the judge
of the Willesden County Court, which is just round the corner,
and there are a lot of people waiting for me to try their cases.
I do not want to be late and keep them waiting." He said:
" You heard what I said, you'll have to wait." There was
nothing else I could do, so I got back into my car and waited.
When he had finished delivering the coal he went to the side of
his lorry and then slowly took a cigarette out of a packet
and slowly lighted it. He then slowly clambered into the
driving seat and sat back and puffed away at his cigarette. His
slowness was quite deliberate. After a short time he turned on
the engine and then very slowly came past my car. As he did
so he looked out of the window and said to me: " Are you in
a hurry? "

Now there is a section of the County Courts Act which
says that anybody who insults the judge, a juror or a witness
while going to or coming from court is guilty of contempt of
court and can be fined or sent to prison. I took the view

that this section referred only to the immediate precincts of the court and, although I was, indeed, going to court and he knew it because I had told him so, this did not fall within the section. If it did, a witness's wife who insulted him on his way to court could be imprisoned or fined. But, supposing I had taken the other view and considered that the man should be proceeded against for contempt of court, how could I have heard the case myself? He might have denied what had happened or given a different account of it from mine. Could I sit in judgment on him and say: " I prefer my account to yours "? Bearing in mind that this is a criminal charge I have no doubt that I could not. The case would have had to be heard by another judge and I should have had to give evidence like any other witness.

The Welsh case went to the Court of Appeal. If I may say so, I think that both that Court and Mr. Justice Lawton were right, the judge in imprisoning some of the offenders in default of undertakings as to their future conduct, and the Court of Appeal in showing mercy and preventing martyrdom, while indicating that future offenders would not be so tenderly treated.

The two most serious criticisms of a judge are bias and abuse of power, but remoteness and lack of imagination can also do harm. It was years before I really started to use my imagination and probably even then I did not use it sufficiently. Here is a simple example. At the present moment in most courts a seat is only offered to a witness in the case of senility, illness or pregnancy. Why? Of course in many cases the witness is only giving evidence for a short time and there is little point in his sitting down. In plenty of other cases a witness prefers to stand. But a friend of mine, who was an expert witness in the High Court, complained to me that he had to spend two hours in the witness-box standing all the time. He would very much have liked to sit down. And so would quite a number of witnesses.

In the United States of America they call it the witness " stand " but witnesses always have a chair. Why was it not until I had been on the Bench for years that I started offering witnesses a seat? Pure lack of imagination. The average judge deserves the reputation for compassion which is given to him by many of those who have written to me. So it is not out of callousness that he lets the witness stand. It has always been done in the past. And he does not think of changing the practice. But it requires no legislation and no alteration of the rules to change it, and I cannot think of any reason for not changing it at once. I should make it plain that there are judges who offer witnesses a seat today but they are in a minority. My remarks, of course, apply to every court where there are witnesses and I hope that steps will be taken to bring this matter to the attention of justices. If the only result of these lectures is that in future all witnesses are offered a seat if they are going to be in the witness-box any length of time, I shall feel I have achieved something.

So people have stood for years through my own and other judges' lack of imagination. But worse than that has happened. For lack of judicial imagination thousands of people who have committed no crime have gone to prison when they should not have gone. No one troubled to think about the matter. Or if they did, they did nothing beyond thinking. I had been over fifteen years on the Bench before I did anything about it. The only thing I can say in my favour is that I did then do something about it. And, had I not done so, another 2,000 innocent people would probably have gone to prison every year.

Let me explain. When imprisonment for debt was said to have been abolished by the Debtors Act 1869 a power was still left to a judge to commit a debtor to prison for a period not exceeding six weeks, if it was proved that since the judgment against him he had had the means to pay the debt or one or more of the instalments ordered. When a debtor was committed to prison on these grounds the court always suspended the order so long as he paid so much a week or so much a month. Before making the committal order judges satisfied themselves that the debtor was in a position to pay, *e.g.* that, after providing for his wife and children, he had sufficient left over.

This imprisonment was *not* for contempt of court, as has sometimes been stated. It was simply a very effective method of forcing a debtor to pay, through the fear of imprisonment. There might be 180,000 of these orders made and approximately 173,000 debtors would find the money somehow, sometimes by stealing it. But it was not because the court was insulted by non-payment that the debtor went to prison. It was solely a weapon given to the creditor and, if the creditor did not want a debtor to go to prison after an order of imprisonment had been made, he could prevent the order from being enforced even though the debtor had paid nothing and even though he had said he would not pay and even though the judge wanted the man to go to prison. The creditor's decision overrode that of the judge. There can be no question of contempt of court in such cases.

In accordance with the recommendation of the Withers Payne Committee this method of enforcing debts will be abolished when the Lord Chancellor, acting under the provisions of the Administration of Justice Act 1970, gives the word, but it was still very much in force at the time of which I am speaking.

Now most debtors are feckless people who are not good at looking after themselves and many of them are inadequate and cannot communicate. A debtor who had been ordered to pay, say, ten shillings a week when he was in work might fall out of work. He could have applied to the judge to suspend the order until he was back in work and, if the judge was satisfied that he was genuinely out of work, the order would have been suspended. But many of these inadequate people did not know how to help themselves. By May 1965 I had been worried for some time about this, knowing that about 400 debtors a month were going to prison and I wondered whether the law was being properly administered. I don't mean that I thought judges had exceeded their jurisdiction or that the committal orders should not have been made with the law as it was then. I simply wondered if debtors were being given a proper opportunity to have these orders suspended in the case of their being ill or thrown out of work or the like. So I obtained permission to visit Brixton prison to interview some debtors. I took with me another judge and my own registrar. The other judge thought that the law as it was then should be maintained. I thought the contrary. I chose him, as I wanted to take someone who was not obviously on the side of the debtors.

We interviewed four debtors and all of us were absolutely satisfied that three of them should not have been in prison at all. Each of the three could have had the order suspended if he had applied to the judge. They simply did not know what to do and just went to prison. As a result of this, the other judge and I wrote to the Lord Chancellor's department, which acted with extreme speed and notified all county courts that bailiffs must explain the position carefully to all debtors whom they arrested. It also arranged for the form given to the debtor to be slightly altered so as to make the position clearer. This was at the end of May 1965. Up to and including that month the average number of debtors going to prison per month was, as I have said, 400. In June 1965 the number dropped dramatically to 200 and remained constant at that figure thereafter. The actual figures were March 481, April 374, May 419, June 238, July 222, August 187. The figure for 1964 was 5,948, for 1965, 3,669, for 1966, 3,155 and for 1967, 3,329.

Except in periods affected by one of the World Wars about 5–6,000 debtors on an average went to prison each year from 1870 onwards. In 1962 the number was nearly 8,000. How many hundreds of county court judges have there been since 1869? And none of us thought of querying the matter. Ours was the chief responsibility. But other people might have thought about it when they saw the published figures of debtors going to prison. Every now and then M.P.s and the Press quite rightly make a fuss because a single person is thought to have been imprisoned wrongly. As far as I know, no one asked a question about the imprisonment of 2,000 innocents a year. I only went into the matter when I was less than three years from retirement and indeed, had I been older, I would have retired before May 1965, as by that time I had done more than fifteen years' service.

What else did I not think of? It is the danger of tradition (which is an excellent servant and a safeguard against unnecessary change) that, if not mastered, it may become master. Because a thing has always happened, we think it should go on happening. I have already pointed out that lawyers are so used to seeing witnesses going in and out of the witness-box that they frequently do not appreciate the state of mind of the witness. It is desirable to put a witness at ease as far as possible. He will never be perfectly at ease in such strange and awesome surroundings but some judges do not take sufficient steps to help the witness. Some indeed go to the other extreme. Here is a comment from a boy who gave evidence.

> " While I was in the witness stand I was continually told to address my remarks to the judge, even though it was the respective counsel asking the questions. The judge seemed to be the least interested person in the room. I was rather nervous, but the judge was of no help at all. On two or three occasions he sharply told me to speak up. I was under the impression that he was unreachable and that I should always feel uneasy when speaking to him, whether on or off duty."

Both counsel and the judge are to blame for part of his complaint. Unless the judge is deaf (in which case he should get a good hearing-aid or retire) it is absurd to expect a witness to look at one person and answer another. The witness is uncomfortable enough as it is. He is facing the judge. A question comes from counsel. It is natural that he should want to turn towards counsel and he should be allowed to do so. When counsel told a witness to " turn to his Honour," I told him that he need not, provided he was audible.

The average witness has never been in a courtroom before and is pretty terrified at the thought, let alone the reality. He comes into court where he sees a bewigged and robed judge on a dais and counsel in wigs and gowns and an usher in a gown. It is the daily round for the legal profession. It is a nightmare for the witness. His name is called and he goes to the witness-box. The usher tells him to take the Bible in his right hand and repeat the words on the card. Perhaps he has not got the right glasses with him or in his nervousness cannot find them in his pocket. Eventually he succeeds in finding them and, wondering if he has committed an offence by being so slow, he looks at the card. He begins:

" I swear by the Almighty God that . . ."

" No," says the usher.

He tries again:

" I swear by the Almighty God . . ."

" No," says the usher and points out that there is no " the." Some witnesses say " the Almighty God " and some " my Almighty God." In many courts it means that they have to start again.

Finally he completes the ordeal and takes an oath which, if he or anyone else thought about it, he has little chance of being allowed to keep. As all lawyers know, it runs as follows:

" I swear by Almighty God that the evidence I shall give shall be the truth, the whole truth and nothing but the truth."

Or, alternatively, if there is an affirmation:

" I, John Jones, do solemnly and sincerely and truly declare and affirm that . . .," etc.

The words " so help me God," which used to appear at the end of the oath, are no longer used. In consequence, a person is made to swear that the evidence he gives will be true when, if he is a reasonably intelligent and honest man, he knows perfectly well that it may not be true, particularly if the events about which he is to speak took place about a year previously. If he believes in God, why should he be compelled to swear by God that he will do something which he knows he may not be able to do? If he asked leave to say, " I swear that I will do my best to tell the truth " he would be refused such leave. Next he is required to swear that his evidence will contain the whole truth. In many cases the laws of evidence will not

permit him to tell the whole truth. Hearsay evidence is normally excluded, not because it is not part of the whole truth
but because it would be dangerous to allow it.

In the High Court (but not in the county court) certain
types of hearsay may today be admitted but, when the witness
takes the oath, he cannot possibly tell whether he will be
allowed to tell the whole truth or not.

If a man who had witnessed an accident and on going home
immediately told his wife all about it, that could be an extremely important part of the whole truth, particularly if the
trial did not take place until many months or some years after,
but no judge in the county court could allow him to say what
he told his wife, even though he had sworn that he would so do.
It is very doubtful if this would be permitted in the High Court
either. Why should a witness be compelled to swear by his
Maker that he will do something that he won't be allowed to
do? Finally, witnesses have to swear that their evidence will
contain nothing but the truth. An honest and intelligent man
knows perfectly well that something which is untrue may creep
into his evidence. He may believe it to be true but it may be
completely false.

It is right that the solemnity of the occasion should be
impressed upon the witness and upon those in court. But
there would be no difficulty in doing this and providing an oath
which the witness could really keep. In Scotland the judge
administers the oath himself and stands up to do so. What
could be the objection to the Scottish practice in that respect
being adopted in England and to the judge rising and saying
to the witness: " Do you swear by Almighty God " (or, if the
witness wishes to affirm, " Do you promise ") " that you will
do your best to tell the truth?" That could be done with
dignity and solemnity.

It would mean something and it would be far less difficult for the witness than having to undergo the present ordeal. He would simply answer " yes " or " I do " and the judge could ensure by the way in which he looked at the witness and said the words that it was a very important occasion.

There is a movement to abolish the oath altogether, partly on the ground that Christ said: " Swear not at all. Let your yea be yea and your nay nay." This is an arguable matter, but, whether the oath itself is retained or not, the wording ought to be changed.

A suggestion made to me was that the oath should be abolished and that instead the judge should ask the witness some such question as this: " Do you know that the law requires you on pain of heavy penalties to give full and honest evidence to the best of your recollection? " and then wait for the witness to say " Yes."

Today, the witness, having got through the oath, is then questioned by counsel and, when he has given his name and address, he is perhaps asked " to cast his mind back to January 17, 1969." By that time many unfortunate witnesses are not in a position to cast their minds backwards or forwards or sideways.

There are witnesses who do not require help from the judge, there are some who would feel aggrieved at receiving it and there are some who are so tensed up that a few words of kindness may reduce them to tears. A judge has to consider the category of each witness going into the box, but in a substantial number of cases it would be helpful if he said to a witness at the beginning of his evidence something like this:

" Now I am quite sure that, whatever I say to you, you are bound to feel uncomfortable, but I want you to feel as relaxed as possible. We lawyers fully understand that

you are not used to being in the witness-box and that
everything may suddenly fly out of your head. If that
happens just say so and we will wait until you have
collected yourself. Don't be frightened to say that you
do not understand the question or to ask for it to be
explained or repeated. And, if you do not remember
something, by all means say so. Would you feel happier
sitting down or standing up?''

I dare say a lot of judges will tell me that this is wholly
unnecessary, that there is no point in spoon-feeding witnesses
and that they have managed very well up to now. Why should
not everything go on as it has before? In my view the fact
that many witnesses have sometimes not been treated in the
past with enough consideration is no reason for not starting
now.

I venture to think that, if every judge treated those witnesses, who looked as though they might benefit from it, in
some such way as I have suggested, the criticisms which I have
had of unkindness and remoteness would not have been made.
And the evidence would have come out in the case at least as
well and probably better.

The same student, who suggested a sabbatical year for
newly appointed judges, also suggested that High Court
judges should be drawn from the ranks of non-lawyers, *e.g.*
from eminent industrialists and trade unionists. While the
use of such laymen as assessors to assist a judge in certain
cases might be of considerable value, it would be quite impossible for a non-lawyer to acquire sufficient knowledge of law
or practice to enable him to preside in an English court so
long as we have our present system or one akin to it.

Another new suggestion was made by an editor, namely,
that in order that judges should be less remote and not in a

cul-de-sac, they should come back and practise at the Bar for a time after a few years on the Bench. I do not imagine that this suggestion would find much favour among the Bar or the Bench. I very much doubt if judges would accept elevation to the Bench if they knew that they subsequently would have to practise at the Bar, even for a comparatively short time before returning to the Bench. Moreover, it is to be hoped that their powers of advocacy might have waned.

Another editor writes that there is a basic impression in Fleet Street that judges are doing a pretty fair and competent job of work but that there is a very deep feeling among the public that they are out of touch with the realities of life in these days of the man on the moon.

I wonder if this is so? A hundred or even fifty years ago the judge's salary enabled him to live on quite a different scale from that on which he lives today. In about 1909 a leading K.C. (who later became Mr. Justice Lush) told a young barrister that on no account must he be seen carrying a parcel, however small, in the Temple. Mr. Justice Lush retired in 1925. When a judge never went by public transport, was never called " ducks " by the conductress and only moved about in moneyed circles, it may be that he had less understanding of popular ideas or popular ways. I am inclined to believe that the frequent comment that modern judges are out of touch with reality is largely based on fiction. There may be a very few older judges today who give the impression that they still live in a pre-war world, but they are disappearing quickly.

Judges' incomes are worth far less than they were in real terms, nearly all of them travel by public transport, many help with the washing-up and most of them have learned from personal experience how the man on the Clapham omnibus lives. Most, if not all of them, have radio and television and have heard of the Beatles even if they do not all listen to them. Physical remoteness in court is desirable and, while a case is proceeding, so is remoteness from those concerned with it, but I doubt if remoteness in thought is a justifiable complaint against the vast majority of judges today. But the remoteness which absolutely inhibits judges from talking to the Press will, it is to be hoped, never disappear.

A few judges may still be a little old-fashioned and one has heard occasionally of judicial complaints about a witness's dress. Such complaints will die out. If a person would be accepted in a church, he or she should be acceptable in a court. Personally I never minded what people wore in my court, provided their apparel was not put on in order to try to lower the dignity of the court. On one occasion, a defendant, who was known apparently as Screaming Lord Sutch, came to my court. I had not the least idea who he was. My clerk told me, but, if necessary, I should have had to ask the question in court. But I don't think the failure to know the names of all pop stars indicated remoteness. Mr. Sutch came to court dressed only in a tiger skin and accompanied by two reporters to see the fun. I asked him if those were the clothes he usually wore and he said that they were. So we got on with the case and there was no fun to report. It seemed to me that it was not my business to dictate to people what they should wear in my court, provided their dress was decent and not intended to bring the court into contempt. If Mr. Sutch usually wore a tiger skin why should I object to his clothes any more than I should object to those of a nun or an Arab? In fact Mr. Sutch turned out to be a very sensible young man, who conducted his case with courtesy and ability.

So much for remoteness. There is little of it and what there is will not last long. The average judge lives like anyone else in the same income bracket, subject to certain restrictions. What is his private life?

Here is what one commentator says: " One has the impression that judges have no private lives but one is comforted by hearing of little indiscretions committed by such people."

It is obvious that a high standard of conduct is required of a judge in his private life, but how strict must he be about this? Plainly he must not visit disorderly houses or striptease shows or entertainments of that kind. There was a High Court judge towards the end of the last century, who was found in a brothel, but at least he had the grace or forethought to be found dead.

The public are entitled to think that those in whom they place so much trust in fact behave themselves. What constitutes behaving oneself? Some activities are obviously ruled out, while it must be left to the good sense of each individual to come to a fair conclusion about border-line cases. One of the finest lawyers in the country used regularly to go to greyhound meetings and, I think, even owned a greyhound. There was nothing illegal or immoral in that. But was it the sort of life which a judge should lead? He was never made a judge, though otherwise eminently fitted for the Bench.

In an article in the *Sunday Express* dated March 9, 1969, which was headlined " The Judge who was too ardent in a taxi," a lady referred to her friendship with a judge—now long since dead—and mentioned the fact that there was " a rather despairing scene in the taxi-cab when he attempted to molest me." She also said that he wanted her to become his mistress, but that she refused to agree. He was already married, so that there could be no question of their marrying. The lady said that, when she left dancing to find a new vocation, this particular judge launched her on her new enterprise and that he bought a hotel for her. The judge was not a High Court judge, but was the equivalent of a county court judge on the criminal side. The interesting thing to note about him is that it was he who behaved so improperly at the Old Bailey in the case to which I referred on pages 71–74. He was not an able lawyer, but he may have been up to the standard of county court judges then being appointed. Whether or not he would have been appointed if he had had the trial run which I have recommended, it is impossible to say. It is only fair to add that, while there appears no reason for not accepting everything that the lady said in the article referred to, the judge himself is not alive to give his version of the story.

One of the problems which the modern age produces for the judge is the motor-car. Plainly it is absurd to say that no judge should drive a car, but, if he does drive a car, he is bound to commit a number of criminal offences, because all motoring offences are criminal offences. Every experienced driver knows that, at the least on a few occasions, he must have driven without due care and attention and anyone who lives in London or a large town is likely from time to time to have committed the offence of obstruction by leaving his car unattended at somewhere other than an authorised parking place or a meter. Very occasionally a judge has been convicted of a motoring offence. One county court judge was convicted of a serious motoring offence and another offence allied to it. He immediately resigned. In none of the other cases was the nature of the offence such as to make this essential.

This must depend to some extent upon the judicial work of the judge. If a Law Lord were convicted of a parking offence, no one in the country would suggest that he should cease to be a Law Lord. If, however, a metropolitan magistrate were regularly convicted of parking offences, I think that there would be grave difficulty in his continuing to sit as a magistrate, as he would be trying such cases himself.

Most, if not all, judges drive with extreme care, because the majority of them try accident cases and realise that it would not look well for their cars to be found hugging a lamp post just after they had criticised Mr. Jones for doing much the same thing. Although from time to time the driving of a judge must fall below the required standard of care, this will happen far less often than in the case of the ordinary motorist. If you like, because they do not want to be caught. There is only one way of being sure that you won't be caught and that is not to do it.

But judges do have ordinary private lives, although they have to be a little more careful than other people in what they do. For example, although there is nothing wrong in going to a public-house, a judge would be ill-advised to go into a West End public-house at night. A fight might take place or he might be assaulted by a prostitute and he might have to give evidence as a witness later on. People who read about the case might think that the judge was a " pub-crawler " and at the least might say that " he liked his little drop." So judges must be careful not to take chances which other people can reasonably take.

Tradition is very helpful to a judge and I do not claim much credit for having resisted temptation on one such occasion. One day, while I was a widower, I received a telephone call. When I answered the telephone an attractive foreign female voice said: " Hullo, va bene ? " " I beg your pardon ? " I said. " It is Angela, the little Italian girl." The things which I regret in life are not the things I have done but the things I have not, and I sometimes wonder what would have happened had I taken advantage of the wrong number to ask

Angela out to tea, but the tradition is so strong that I never even considered it. It must be remembered that, even if Angela were a most discreet girl and no one else had known about the encounter, one person besides me would have known about it—Angela.

But apart from these small restrictions most judges lead a normal happy life. The great majority are married and marriage for most people is the foundation of happiness.

I think I should now say something about judges' holidays. High Court judges get something over thirteen weeks' holiday in the year. Some county court judges get thirteen weeks, some rather less and a few considerably less. Stipendiary magistrates only get six weeks, but they usually get one free day in the working week as well, or at least they are supposed to do so.

I have received complaints that judges' holidays are far too long and that they could do their work with far less. So they could, but how well would they do it? A judge normally sits from 10.30 a.m. till 4.15 or 4.30 p.m., with an interval of an hour or less for lunch. During the whole of the time that he sits in court he has to listen to every single word that is said, and, when witnesses are giving evidence, to observe the way in which they give it. In a case where the issues are simple, the concentrated attention which the judge has to give is a very considerable strain upon him, but in many cases the issues are not so simple, and in some cases difficult points of law are involved. Then the strain is even greater.

It is very important that every judge should be on top of his job, that he should be courteous and patient and in full command of his intellectual faculties. I have already commented on the fact that possibly some judges do not appreciate the difficulties of a witness in giving evidence and do not give him sufficient help. Patience and courtesy are very important but they may not be enough. In my opinion, if judges' holidays were cut down, there would be less patience and less courtesy and less chance of a judge fully understanding the difficulties of a witness. A judge should come into court fresh and ready for the heavy strain that is imposed upon him every day. Unless he does this, the standard of justice will decline, a witness's ordeal will be even greater and a judge's decision will be more likely to be wrong.

Whatever sort of judge I was, I can say that during my whole eighteen years I was always physically and mentally as well equipped as I could be to do the job to the best of my ability. If my holidays had been cut in two, I feel sure I would have been that much worse. Obviously, in those circumstances, one would try harder and to begin with no difference might be noticed. In the same way a man who has been up all night will have to make a special effort to do his work the next day. By reason of the special effort he may do it as well as he normally does, but he could not keep on that way.

Personally, I think that justice is such a precious commodity that everything reasonable should be done to attain the highest standard. It will always be far from perfect in every country, but most countries look up to English justice. That is mainly due to the integrity and ability of our judges. Their integrity will in no way be affected by a reduction in their holidays, but their ability to conduct cases to the best advantage of the public would in my view certainly be affected. But, if the public does not want to pay for the more expensive article, it can have the cheaper.

Obviously, if holidays were only slightly cut down the difference might be minimal, but the danger is that, once the idea of reducing judges' holidays has been acted on, it may be done again and again, just as income tax was gradually raised. The difference in judicial behaviour and ability may at first be so small that it will not be noticed but in the end, say, after thirty years of alteration, the picture of a judge (in the words of one of my schoolboy correspondents) as " an aged man in wig and gown, suffering from gall-stones and fever, surrounded by aged clerks and very old books " might become the true one. He would not be older but he would age much quicker. The Beeching Report suggests that the Long Vacation should be shortened and judges' holidays staggered, but not shortened. That would be a purely administrative problem, and it is a good idea if it can work. But it does create serious problems for barristers and solicitors.

Before leaving the private lives of judges I ought to say something about divorce. Although the law will be different from January 1971, adultery will still be a ground for divorce from the practical point of view. There have been judges in the last forty years who have been divorced on the grounds of adultery *before* their appointment. This is a troublesome matter and personally I do not think it was dealt with as it should have been. It is true that things have changed a good deal since I was called to the Bar in 1923. I had an action during the 1920s between a married man and his ex-mistress. The judge who tried the case said: " How can I believe either of these parties because they admit that they were living together in adultery? "

Even in the 1920s that seemed to me to be going a bit far, but, on the other hand, where a case is being tried today by a judge and the question is whether he should believe the plaintiff or the defendant, it is legitimate for counsel for either party to cross-examine the other to suggest that he has committed adultery in the past. In legal language, this is said to " go to his credit." Because a man has committed adultery it does not necessarily mean that he is a liar, but it is a fact that a judge is entitled to take into consideration. Suppose that judge had had a finding of adultery against him before his appointment. It would be embarrassing for counsel to put the question, and one side or the other might think, quite wrongly, that the judge's own past experience might affect the result of the case.

Obviously my opinion is not shared by everyone or the appointments would not have been made. It may be that I have not put into the balance sufficiently the loss to the public if those appointments had not been made.

A judge has to take great care that no one can suggest that he has decided in favour of a party because he knew him or his advocate or because of some information given to him by one party in the absence of the other. It is nearly fifty years since it was alleged in a magazine that a county court judge used to decide cases in favour of a barrister friend of his. The barrister ceased to appear in front of him and nothing of the kind has ever happened since.

A judge will never try a case if he is aware that he knows one of the parties even slightly. I was upset when I learned that I had granted a divorce in an undefended case to a man who was a great friend of my sister-in-law. I had not the faintest idea who he was or I would never have tried the case. But, though a judge will not hear a case if he is acquainted with either of the parties, he is often bound to know the advocates who appear before him and sometimes one may be a friend of his. Occasionally a son has appeared in front of a father and possibly a father has appeared in front of his son. This sort of thing is inevitable, whatever the legal structure. And it is no doubt due to the unblemished reputation for integrity which judges enjoy that, except for the case of nearly fifty years ago, no complaint, as far as I know, has ever been made on this score. Nevertheless a good deal of care has to be exercised lest a litigant—quite wrongly—should get the idea that he has been unfairly prejudiced. Most people know that a judge always discloses any interest, however small, which he may have in a company concerned in a case which he is about to try, and offers not to try it. If his interest were more than minimal he could refuse to try it.

The outgoing judge of the court where I sat for many years invited me to come and see him before I took over. When I went into his room I found that he had with him the solicitor who did most of the work in that court. He introduced me to him and said he would be of great help to me. Naturally I said nothing at the time, but the judge's behaviour showed a complete lack of understanding of the position. This solicitor often appeared against litigants in person, he did most of the judgment summonses (applications to send debtors to prison) and he was employed as agent by many outside solicitors. What was a judgment debtor to think if the solicitor appearing against him was closeted with the judge for half-an-hour or more? The solicitor in question was a man of great ability and absolute integrity and he conducted his cases efficiently and fairly, but after my first introduction to him I never saw him again by himself until by accident we met many miles from the court while on holiday. I was very pleased to have the opportunity of telling him why I might have appeared to be rather unfriendly after the judge's friendly introduction. He fully understood. The judge was a man of complete integrity and his conduct was simply due to a lack of imagination.

County court judges in the country must sometimes have difficult problems of this kind if they become close friends of local advocates. Will the litigant in person think he has had a fair deal if he subsequently sees the judge and the opposing advocate shooting together? In fact the judge's problem in such a case is to see that he does not lean too far backwards and do injustice to his advocate friend's client.

Sometimes during a case the judge visits the scene of an accident with the parties and their representatives. It is of great importance on such occasions that he should never allow one advocate to be next to him when the other is out of earshot. It is not the lawyers concerned in the case who will be anxious about this sort of thing, it is the parties who may very well be upset by something that happens. " What did Brown's counsel say to the judge when we went to look at the house? " says Jones. And if Jones loses the case, he may (quite wrongly) imagine that it was because of what took place on that occasion.

I now want to deal with quite a different aspect of accidents. Most of the time of the judges in the Queen's Bench Division is taken up today with cases of accidents on the road or in the factory. At the moment I am only concerned with those on the road. How real are these decisions? There have been cases where a judge has said that he has been unable to make up his mind, whereupon the Court of Appeal has politely told him that he must.

Well, of course, you can toss a coin mentally to decide whether the plaintiff or the defendant was over the white line, but it hardly seems a satisfactory way of deciding the issue. I once tried a case [2] where damages for fraud were claimed. The evidence took a long time and I listened to it as carefully as I could. In the end I said this. If the plaintiff has to prove his case as surely as he would have to prove it in a criminal court, then in my view he fails. In other words, I am not satisfied of the fraud beyond all reasonable doubt, but, if the

[2] *Hornal* v. *Neuberger* [1957] 1 Q.B. 247.

plaintiff only has to show that there was probably a fraud, I am satisfied that there probably was. Two members of the Court of Appeal very politely suggested that I was being too meticulous and said in effect that, if I thought that the defendant was probably guilty I should have gone the whole hog and said he was certainly guilty. (I suspect that most women would say the same.)

Were the two Lords Justices right? A person accused of a crime has to have his guilt proved beyond all reasonable doubt. There are a great many accident cases tried by judges where, if the question were whether the defendant had been guilty of careless driving under the criminal law, the judge might say he was not quite satisfied, but where he is able to say that the probability is that the defendant was guilty. That is enough to decide the issue in a civil case. And there is a considerable difference between being satisfied beyond reasonable doubt and being satisfied on the probabilities.

A judge should not be forced to say " I think this " or " I think that " when he doesn't really think it. Some accident cases are simple but some are far from simple. Normally it is only the less simple which come to court. Many accidents have taken place long before the case is heard. The result of the case will depend upon many imponderables. Was the plaintiff knocked so hard on the head that he remembers nothing? Were there any witnesses? At the date of the trial, perhaps a year or more after the event, can they really remember what happened? Mr. Justice Macnaghten used to say that the courts were full of honest witnesses whose memories, as time passed, became more and more certain and less and less accurate. Then, did the police take statements? Were the people from whom those statements were taken really in a condition to make them? Did they really understand what they were saying? Were the witnesses of the accident really independent? Did the person who heard a bang and looked up eventually come to the conclusion that he'd seen the whole of the accident from beginning to end? How good are the solicitors on each side in preparing cases for trial? If experts are called about the state of the vehicles or the nature of the damage, how good are they? How good are the respective counsel who conduct such cases and how good is the judge at deciding them?

Most judges drive cars. Should a judge be disqualified from hearing a case (*a*) if he drives, (*b*) if he does not drive? Is it better for him to come to the case without any prejudices of any kind? There are many more questions one can ask in considering whether the judge's decision is likely to be right. In some cases how can it be except by accident? It is almost fair to adapt W. S. Gilbert's song about the heavy dragoon to the decision in an accident case:

" Take of these elements all that is fusible,

Melt them all down in a pipkin or crucible,

Set them to simmer and take off the scum

And a judge's decision's the residuum."

If and when eventually judges appear in the highest court of all and are asked this question: " In how many cases where you said you believed a particular witness did you really believe him or did you only say it because it was the only way of deciding the case? ", what will they reply? The answers would be interesting.

We cannot look into the hearts or minds of men. We can look at their demeanour in the witness-box (which, having regard to the comparatively short time we see them there and the nervousness from which they may be suffering, may not be altogether a true guide to where the truth lies), we read the correspondence and the other documents, we hear all the other evidence in the case and we can usually form a reasonable judgment as to what would ordinarily happen in similar circumstances, and that is about the best we can do. It is true that some witnesses show by their demeanour that they are not telling the truth, but by no means are all liars so helpful.

I once had a witness who gave a pretty unsatisfactory account of himself in cross-examination. So eventually I asked him a few questions and his answers were not much better. So I then said: " Look, Mr. So-and-So, you were a Customs officer, were you not, before you retired? " " I was." " And, in that capacity, sometimes you asked passengers about their luggage and they told you lies in answer to your questions? " " Yes." " Then sometimes you asked them further questions and they lost their heads and said anything that came into them, true or false? " " Yes," he said, and added: " like I'm doing now."

And another similar witness whom I questioned answered unsatisfactorily, so I said to him: " Look, Mr. So-and-So, if you'd been the judge and I'd been the witness and I'd answered your questions as you've answered mine, what would you have thought? " " I'd have been a bit dubious," he said.

Some judges have said to me that they are satisfied they can usually tell whether a witness is telling the truth or not from the way in which he gives his evidence. Their powers of observation are better than mine.

The following story well illustrates the difficulty which I certainly found in judging a man's character simply from his appearance.

I had finished my list one day when I was asked if I would re-try a case which another judge in my court had tried. This occasionally happens when something untoward has taken place during the trial of the case by the other judge. For example he may have accidentally been told something that he ought not to have been told until he had decided the case, *e.g.* how much money the defendant had paid into court or something of that sort. So one never asks the reason for a re-trial.

The action arose out of a motor car accident. The plaintiff said he was driving in the middle of a long line of traffic which was stopping and starting. He had been stationary for about a quarter of a minute when he was run into from behind by the defendant. The defendant denied this entirely. He said that the only truthful thing that the plaintiff had said was that they were in that road at that time and that there was a collision. What happened, he said, was this. Both cars were parked by the side of the road and the plaintiff presumably wanted to drive on but couldn't do so because of a car in front of him. So, in order to be able to get out, he backed into the defendant's car, which was stationary.

I must say that I preferred the evidence of the plaintiff to that of the defendant and the extent of the damage suggested that the collision had probably occurred in the way described by the plaintiff rather than as described by the defendant. But the defendant called an independent witness. This was a young man aged about thirty who said he had been standing by the side of the road and had seen the accident, and that it happened as the defendant had said. He seemed a decent young man and said that he did not know the plaintiff or the defendant before the accident. I still had a feeling that the plaintiff was in the right, but quite obviously, if this witness was an ordinary independent witness, I could not have said that the plaintiff had proved his case in the light of this evidence. But when a completely independent witness, who was not driving a car or a bicycle but was merely standing on the pavement, gives evidence, I always want to be sure that he really has seen the accident. I also want to be sure that he is not a person who rather enjoys giving evidence. There are a few people—a very few—who give in their names after an accident because they like the idea of giving evidence. So I asked the young man if he had ever given evidence before and he said that he had done so once when he himself was in the position in which the plaintiff claimed to have been.

> " But, apart from that occasion and this occasion, you have never been in court before in your life? " I asked.
>
> " Must I answer that question? " he said.
>
> " Why don't you want to? " I asked.
>
> " Because I've got a record."
>
> " What for? "
>
> " Oh, burglary and housebreaking."
>
> " How many convictions?"
>
> " Oh, about eight."

I subsequently discovered that the reason why the case had been sent to me to re-try was this. The other judge was rather quicker off the mark than I was and, after he had heard the plaintiff and defendant give their version of the accident, he said: " I find for the plaintiff." Whereupon the defendant said: " But you haven't heard my independent witness." The judge realised he could not properly hear the independent witness at that stage and so he sent the case to me to re-try.

But the interesting thing was this. I subsequently heard from the registrar, though naturally I didn't know it at the time, that the other judge after adjourning the case had said this: " I saw his independent witness. Didn't like the look of him at all. A burglar or something." And this merely from seeing the man in court. I certainly had not that judge's powers of observation.

I have not said all this for the purpose of self-criticism or of criticising other judges who try accident cases. I have said it because I think that the time has come to abolish these cases, at any rate, where there are personal injuries. In a sense everyone uses the roads. Even a person who is bedridden has food and help brought to his side by road. Therefore everyone is in a sense responsible for the accidents which take place. No one has an accident on purpose and therefore the country as a whole is responsible for the thousands of deaths and hundreds of thousands of injuries which take place each year. The country as a whole, therefore, should pay compensation to those affected, whether or not negligence is proved in any person. It is absurd that compensation for the loss of a leg in a road accident should depend upon whether enough of the " scum " was removed before the judge arrived at his " residuum." (See the verse on page 119).

Compensation should be paid partly by insurance companies, partly by the public at large. This has been recommended in the report of a Royal Commission (the Woodhouse Report) in New Zealand. It may well be that the same course should be taken with regard to accidents in factories and possibly also in the home, but the considerations in those cases are rather different. In any event one has to start somewhere and I suggest that plainly road accidents should come first. Obviously, if the law were so changed it would be provided that a person who deliberately had an accident should be disentitled to compensation. But there would not be many of these, as the danger of the money going to the next-of-kin would be too great for most people who contemplated the idea.

The amount of damages to be recovered might still be left

to the courts to decide or it could be left to one of the Social Security tribunals or the like. If accident cases were taken away from the ordinary courts it would certainly relieve them of much congestion and the present number of judges could comfortably cope with the remaining cases, but I should make it plain that that is not the reason for my suggestion. I think it wrong that a person who has been injured in a road accident should have to go through the present rather hit-or-miss procedure and that he may in the end, after months of waiting, miss. The relief to congestion would save the Lord Chancellor from the difficult task (envisaged by the Beeching Report) of finding another forty satisfactory judges.

One more word about accidents, although my mentioning it may constitute an abuse of power, for writers and lecturers can abuse their power almost as much as judges.

It does not appear that legislation or heavy penalties will prevent accidents. There are not enough police to enforce the law and people do not think that they will be caught. The breathalyser Act merely kept vehicles off the road for a time. Anything which keeps vehicles off the road naturally reduces accidents. But motorists will not stay off the roads for long. What is required is to convince the public that all that is necessary is a little extra care shown by all sections of the public—motorists, mothers of children, pedestrians and everyone else. Why not a national No Accident Day preceded by three or four weeks of propaganda on television, radio, the Press, in the schools, churches, and so on, leading up to this one day on which it should be a point of honour among all members of the population not to be involved in an accident? If on that one day the accident rate dropped it would have proved to the population all that was necessary to reduce the accident rate. That would be a first step. It may be

remembered that the admirable propaganda in October/
November 1969 must have done a great deal to reduce the
accident rate on Guy Fawkes Day in that year.

I shall now refer to an accident case which, in my view,
resulted in a serious injustice in the Court of Appeal. It was
not an appeal from one of my judgments.

Lack of imagination can be found in high places, even in
the Court of Appeal. The object of every court must be to do
justice within the law. Admittedly the law sometimes forces
an unjust decision. If there is no way around it, it is for
Parliament to alter the law if the injustice merits an alteration.
In case someone says that every injustice merits an alteration,
I must point out that this is not the case. We have to have a
set of rules for governing our relationship with the state and
with each other. These rules are the law, but it has been
found beyond the wit of man to devise rules which can be
applied to every occasion. The permutations and combinations in human affairs are infinite and even computers will be
unable to secure perfection. In consequence cases must arise
in every country which the law has not contemplated and every
now and then an instance of injustice will occur. This is quite
inevitable, but sometimes to alter the law to prevent that one
injustice occurring again might cause even more injustice in
other cases. In consequence, Parliament cannot always
remedy every injustice. Where there are men there will
always be examples of human injustice.

Nevertheless, when the courts see an obvious injustice
about to be done to somebody, they usually try to avoid it if
possible, but sometimes, when this could be done if the judges
used their imagination sufficiently, they fail to do this. Just
because something has always been done in a particular way
they cannot think beyond that way. I can at least say in my

own favour that the argument " This has never been done
before, your Honour " did not prevent my doing it if it seemed
the right thing to do and within the law—if only just within.

Here to my mind is an example of an avoidable injustice,
and it occurred in the Court of Appeal in October 1969. The
facts were as follows.

A was seriously injured by the careless driving of B in
1960. B's liability to pay damages to A was never in dispute.
Nevertheless when A sued B for damages, his claim was
eventually dismissed because of his inordinate delay in pur-
suing it. He did not issue his writ until 1963 and, even after
starting proceedings, he let them go to sleep until July 1968
and he refused during this period to follow his own solicitor's
advice to give the necessary information to enable the claim
to be pursued. Why did he behave so curiously and against
his own interests? A psychiatrist reported that the accident
had also affected A's personality and that his behaviour
(wholly unreasonable in the case of a normal person) was
caused by his neurotic condition, which in turn was caused by
the accident.

The court held that this could not be taken into account
and that A had to be treated as though he were a normal
person. It was argued for A that, as B did not dispute liability
to pay damages, he was not prejudiced by the delay. The court
said that the assessment of the amount of the damages had
been rendered much more difficult by the delay and that, had
B's insurance company been given the necessary information,
they would no doubt have paid a sum into court to dispose of
the claim.

All this was very true, but what the court did not appear to
try to do was to see how it could do justice to A without doing
injustice to B's insurers. Plainly it was a grave injustice to A,

both of whose thighs had been broken by B's bad driving, to give him no damages, but it was also true that B's insurers had been put in grave difficulty about assessing the value of A's claim by reason of the delay and the absence of the necessary information.

The way in which the case came before the court was that eventually B's insurers applied to have the action dismissed on the ground of the inordinate delay and the Court of Appeal dismissed it, thereby depriving A of his admitted right to damages arising from the serious injury done to him by B. What seems to have occurred to nobody is that A could have been permitted to continue his action against B on two conditions. First, that he should, of course, indemnify B's insurers against all the costs thrown away. Secondly, that his damages should be limited to a sum of £X, £X being the *lowest* sum which A would have been likely to recover if he had pursued his action in the normal way. Obviously this sum might be much too low, but it would be far better for A to have too little than nothing at all. And there should have been no real difficulty in fixing this sum. Indeed, the defendant's insurers could themselves have suggested it.

If this course had been adopted, what possible injustice could have been done to B? His insurers would have had to pay no more than the minimum which they would have had to pay had the action proceeded in the normal way, and they would have had the use of the money for many years. This seems to me a simple and just solution to the problem.

I can only imagine that it was not adopted because no one ever thought of it, and because it would have been a unique order to make. I certainly have never heard of damages being limited in this way, but it would surely have been possible for the court, as a matter of discretion, to make it a condition of permitting A to continue with his action, that, when he recovered damages against B, he should only enter judgment for the minimum sum, namely, £X.

Incidentally this method of deciding the matter would have disposed of it there and then, as no doubt B's insurers would have immediately paid £X (less the costs) to A and that would have been an end of the matter. As it was, a serious avoidable injustice was done to A, whose extraordinary behaviour may have been caused by B's careless driving.

In my final lecture I shall start by dealing with sentences by judges and in doing so I shall refer to the Great Train Robbery.

CHAPTER 4

THE LESSER JUDGES

I NOW come to the important matter of judges' sentences,
sentences made necessary by the prevalence of crime. There is
little judges can do about crime. It is a pity that those who
could do something about it do not. If the Government (or
Opposition) appreciates that at the present moment this
country is involved in a war against crime, neither of them has
the courage or foresight to deal with the situation properly,[1]
any more than the Government before the 1939–45 war was
prepared to deal with German rearmament. Neither legislation nor heavy sentences will prevent crime. Everyone agrees
that prevention is better than cure but no one will take the
only steps essential to prevent crime. Things are far worse in
the United States of America. Women cannot walk alone at
night in New York. That situation may come to England.
Plenty of police and a strong likelihood of detection are the
antidotes to crime.

There is only one thing to be done. If there were an

[1] This was written before the 1970 General Election but unfortunately it
requires no alteration.

129

international war, the government of the day would see that we had all the men and munitions possible to protect ourselves. But it appears to require an international war to get any real action out of any government. The only method to combat the steadily increasing wave of crime in this country is to put the police force on a proper basis. They are under strength now and they should be at least double their present maximum strength. This can only be done by doubling their pay and otherwise improving their conditions of service. The police force should be able to compete with every other occupation for entrants. It should be much more difficult to get into it. But the rewards of admission should be considerable. The slight rises in pay every now and then are almost valueless. Something drastic has to be done. Neither Government nor Opposition appears to realise that the heavy cost would be worthwhile. They are terrified of the Treasury and of other demands for increase of wages. And perhaps also of being accused of making the country into a police state. That is nonsense. A police state is a country where the government can arrest anyone of whom it disapproves, law-abiding or not. It is a country where personal freedom depends on the whim of the government and not, as here, on the rule of law and a democratically elected Parliament. A great improvement in the numbers of the police force and the qualifications for entry can only benefit the law-abiding public. The political parties talk about law and order but will not take the one courageous but vital step to ensure it. There was a time when a policeman was normally available on beat duty in every part of a town. He would keep order, and help, comfort and protect the public. Where is he now? In how many streets today will a cry for help produce it?

So the depleted police force will have to go on trying to

catch criminals—with steadily decreasing success. This is no fault of the police; without numbers they can do no more than they are doing. And those criminals who are caught and convicted will come before the courts for sentence. I am now only dealing with serious crime for which heavy sentences are likely to be imposed.

Probably no court has sufficient information before it to enable it to pass the appropriate sentence, except in the case of petty offences. In sentencing a person convicted of crime the priorities are as follows:

    (1) The protection of the public as a whole.

    (2) The assistance of any particular individual injured by the crime. Should such a person's feelings be taken into consideration when passing sentence?

    (3) The reformation of the convicted person.

    (4) Retribution, if it is necessary in the public interest.

A very important part of (1) is the protection of individual members of the public who may be injured when the convicted person is at large again. It is not of a great deal of use to send a man to prison for, say, four years for attempted rape if at the end of it he comes out and commits the full crime.

A much more difficult question is whether the desire of the public and of any aggrieved person for revenge or retribution, should in any way affect the sentence. It can be argued that the outraged feelings of the public or an individual should sometimes be solaced in this way but if they should not, some step ought to be taken to alleviate the suffering of an aggrieved person who might be made psychologically and permanently ill in default of such assistance. A mother whose child is gravely injured or killed and who sees the culprit led gently away into a comfortable hospital might be gravely affected for the rest of her life, unless immediate steps are taken to prevent this. It must be recognised that in some cases, whatever steps might be taken, nothing very useful could be done, but the effect of a crime upon an innocent person appears to be a matter which is too seldom taken into consideration.

I think and hope that the day will come when sentences for serious crimes will not be solely in the hands of a judge. It is quite impossible for a judge to be sufficiently informed about the proper sentence for many prisoners. He can only do his best on the material in front of him and his best may not be good enough.

In my opinion either sentences should be passed by a panel (consisting of, say, a doctor, a social worker and a lawyer) or, alternatively, the judge's sentence should be reviewed by such a panel, which should have power to alter the sentence in any way, up or down. (I am expressing no firm view as to the form of such a panel and it may well be that a different constitution would be better.)

Before a satisfactory sentence can be passed there ought to be many interviews between the prisoner and one or more members of the panel, so that they can try to understand what makes him tick the wrong way. What are his hopes and fears? Why did he commit the crime? And so on. It is quite impossible for a judge to do this properly either personally or through the agency of probation officers. There is no time. It must be a slow process. The less serious crimes should be dealt with in the same way, as soon as there is the necessary organisation to deal with them.

Admittedly there are criminals whose intelligence and ability to communicate are so limited that nothing useful is likely to result from such interviews, but that is no reason for not trying. Similarly there are others whose hatred of society is so deep that probably nothing can eradicate it. But at least they will be able to see a change of attitude on the part of authority. I have met some of the dangerous men who are imprisoned in the experimental prison at Grendon and they certainly appear to react well to more understanding treatment.

Such panels should also do what they can to help anyone injured or affected by the crime.

A very important power which the panel ought to have in the case of crimes of violence is to order that the offender be detained, like the inmates of Broadmoor, indefinitely until either the panel or some other body certifies that it is reasonably safe to let him loose on the public again. It is very wrong that, for example, sex maniacs who are not actually certifiable and who cannot restrain their sexual impulses to attack children should be released after their sentences, however long, unless an appropriate committee has certified that it is reasonably safe to do so. It is equally wrong that criminals who are prepared to band together to rob with violence should be released until it is safe to release them.

Suitable establishments should be built where such dangerous people can be detained securely. They should have interesting work, reasonable entertainment, and as much contact as possible with their relatives and the outside world. They should have some hope of fulfilment of life within the establishment's walls. It may be, for some reason which medical science has not yet discovered, that it is through no fault of their own that these people have these dangerous tendencies. This would entitle them to great sympathy, but members of the public whom they are likely to attack must be protected from them.

One day, perhaps, a government will be found which has the courage to repeal the Prisons Act of 1877, which provides that most of the proceeds of sale of prison sites shall go to the local authority. The government could then sell certain prison sites to property developers, and use the money for building establishments where people who are a danger to the public could be housed in humane conditions.

I do not think that any of the local authorities concerned show these reversions in their accounts, so that it would be no serious injustice to them to take away their right to receive the money. No doubt there would be other serious problems in changing the site of a prison, but presumably those problems could be solved, as the only reason given by Lord Gardiner, when Lord Chancellor, for not " blowing up " some of the old prisons is the Act to which I have referred.

The other day a burglar of nineteen tried to rape a woman in the course of committing a burglary. He said: " I don't know what came over me. I get these fits. When I saw the woman I had a sudden urge. I put pressure on her throat to try to stop her fighting. She went unconscious and I ran out of the room." He was sentenced to prison for thirty months with an additional six months for being in breach of a twelve months' conditional discharge which had been imposed upon him earlier for another burglary. The Chairman told the accused: " It was a wicked thing you did that night. You were overcome by lust, and the consequences of your attack on this lady are incalculable."

With respect to the Chairman, what was the use of this homily, and what is the use of this sentence? If this young man of nineteen is going to " get these fits " in the future, the effect upon some other woman may also be incalculable. If justice to the public were done, a man of that kind would be detained until it was certified that it was reasonably safe to let him loose. The young man may indeed deserve sympathy, he may have been brought up in very difficult conditions, very likely he came from a broken home or an institution, he may suffer from some psychological disease, and so on. It is possible (and I hope) that some form of treatment may cure him, but I have at least equal sympathy for the unfortunate woman whom he tried to rape, and possibly even more sympathy for his next victim in twenty or thirty months' time, if he is still going to " get these fits."

Most criminals come from broken homes and many have not had a fair opportunity of leading an honest life. I am glad that a far more enlightened view of the treatment of criminals is now starting to prevail. Many of them may suffer from a sickness which is worse than a physical sickness because it is more difficult to diagnose and treat. I am all in favour of non-violent prisoners being kept in prison for as short a time as possible and on release being helped as much as possible to lead ordinary lives as ordinary members of the community. These are matters with which the sentencing panel to which I have referred would be far better able to deal than a judge.

But at the moment such panels do not exist and, when a judge has to sentence people who are guilty of grave crimes of violence, he has the knowledge that the people being sentenced will eventually be released, whether they are sentenced to life imprisonment or to many years of imprisonment. His main object is to protect the public from their dangerous behaviour. One of the most striking examples of this was the Great Train Robbery.

There are still people who sympathise with the men convicted in the Great Train Robbery case. " After all," they say, " they were only robbing a bank or the equivalent. It was a brilliant idea. It almost came off." I have often heard admiration expressed for these men. What such admirers forget is that these robbers were prepared to use violence if necessary and, if the postmen in charge of the money had not very sensibly held up their hands, they might have been treated as roughly as the unfortunate engine-driver. People are so excited at the idea of getting away with two and a half million pounds that they entirely forget the engine-driver who, in trying to carry out his duty, suffered very grievously. He is now dead. Whether or not his life was shortened by the treatment which he received, it certainly appears that he did not live happily from the time of the occurrence. People also forget that the men were obviously ready and willing to use as much violence as was necessary to carry out their purpose. Is it seriously suggested that men who had spent so much money and thought in preparing their plan and had armed themselves with weapons would have quietly gone away without using those weapons if they had met with resistance? Look at what happened to the one man who did resist. (And now we have a plea that, although the engine-driver was struck down, his worst injury was when he hit his head as he fell. Who was responsible for that?)

No doubt the judge had in mind that it would be a grave temptation to other similar men to try to emulate the example of the train robbers if after a few years' imprisonment they could come out and enjoy the spoils. It must be remembered that most, if not all, of these men have been in prison before. It must also be remembered that only 10 per cent. of the money stolen has ever been recovered. It was as though they wanted to leave a tip for the waiter. As gratuities appear to be on the increase, perhaps next time they will leave 15 per cent.

Judges never have the opportunity of explaining the reasons for what they have done. This is as well, as otherwise there could be a debate between the judge and members of the public after every controversial case. On the other hand, it sometimes does the judge an injustice. " How terrible," some people say, " to put those men away for twenty years or more, when people who commit murder get less." Murder is not necessarily the most serious crime. Attempted murder, for example, or grave assaults can be worse, when the victim may suffer pain for the rest of his shortened life. But the fact that a man may be released early from a sentence for murder does not seem to me to be any good reason for releasing too soon someone who has committed a very grave crime of violence. It may be safe from the public's point of view to release, after only a short time in prison, a man of good character who has murdered his wife in a fit of temper. It will seldom be safe to release a man whose history shows a determination to rob with violence. The sentences imposed on the train robbers may not prove a sufficient deterrent to other resolute criminals but it will at least ensure that the dangerous men who took part in that crime will have no similar opportunity for many years.

In saying this I am in no way going back on what I said earlier. It may well be that all the train robbers, or some of them, fall within the category of people who need treatment rather than punishment. Some or all of them may deserve great sympathy, either because they have some at present undiagnosable malformation of the brain-cells or because they were rejected by society at an early age. But the safety of the public must come first and, until we get proper establishments where such people can live in decency and dignity and, if possible, be cured of their disease, a judge has no alternative to passing very long sentences of imprisonment on such dangerous men for the protection of the public. One can only hope that the more enlightened views about the treatment of criminals will speedily become more prevalent among all sections of society and that it may not be long before a safe alternative is produced to cooping-up these men in objectionable conditions in top-security prisons.

So much for the sentencing power of High Court judges. I now come to the 21,000 justices who form a most important part of the judicial system. In view of their number, it is obviously impossible for me to deal with them in the detailed way in which I dealt with the professional judges, but I shall show how and from among whom justices are appointed, I shall deal with some of the criticisms which are made about the system of appointment and the way in which they carry out their duties and I shall refer to the costs of appeals.

A typical comment which I have received about the system of appointment is as follows:

" J.P.s receive no salary and are therefore all from middle or upper class backgrounds. They also tend to come from amongst the ranks of headmasters, estate agents, etc. because only such people can afford to spend the necessary time in court. This is clearly unfortunate and no doubt leads to many working-class people feeling that they have little chance of justice or understanding from such people. Apart from this, although the justice of the peace may be a man of impeccable character and great understanding, he receives no real legal training. The only preparation deemed necessary is a handful of lectures and a few hours in court. Although he has the clerk of the court to help him on points of law, it is difficult to see how a newly appointed J.P. can be suitable for the job. Thus it is clear that although it would mean the expenditure of considerably more money by the Government or the local

authority, men should receive legal training specifically
to become justices and be suitably paid."

In fact, 5 to 6 per cent. of justices are wage-earners and
the number is increasing. The Civil Service and nationalised
industries allow employees up to twelve days' paid leave a
year to serve as justices and some firms make similar allowances.

Justices come from every walk of life and from most
professions, trades and occupations, except normally that of
the law. But obviously it is much more difficult for someone
in a job to accept the appointment. It may well be that the
time will come when compensation for loss of wages will be
given to enable the constitution of Benches to be even broader-
based than it is at present. As far as possible justices are
chosen so that the Benches do not contain pronounced
majorities with the same political leanings.

I do not personally think that too much (if any) training is
good for a justice. Unless he is as fully trained as a stipendiary
magistrate, he will suffer from the danger of having some, but
not enough, knowledge. Justices are always advised by a
legally qualified clerk and, if they were half-trained, the time
might come when there would be disputes about matters of
law between the qualified clerk and one of the justices. Fur-
thermore, if too much training were required, fewer people
would be available to sit and it would make it still more
difficult for wage-earners to be appointed. The answer to the
criticism that by reason of lack of legal knowledge a justice is
not fit for the job is that for hundreds of years he has with the
assistance of his clerk discharged his duties with a very high
degree of success. People who point to unsatisfactory decisions
may not appreciate that over the years justices try millions of
cases. The percentage of which complaint is made is trifling.

Justices are appointed by the Lord Chancellor except in Lancashire, where they are appointed by the Chancellor of the Duchy of Lancaster. In each case the appointment is made on behalf of the Sovereign. Although they are unpaid, they may receive certain small allowances.

They must be of good character and normally under sixty on appointment. The method of appointment is to obtain the recommendation of an Advisory Committee. Every county and borough has such an Advisory Committee, and the secretary's name and address is made public. The reason that the names of the Committee are not normally known is in order to avoid their being canvassed by prospective candidates for appointment.

Justices appointed after January 1, 1966, have to undergo a course of basic training. Part of this training consists of sitting in court and the other part consists of instruction by lectures and includes visits to penal establishments. After the age of seventy a justice goes on to the supplemental list, unless he is a chairman or deputy-chairman of quarter sessions or has held high judicial office. Once he is on the supplemental list a justice is confined to performing minor administrative functions only. Of the 21,000 justices just over 4,000 are on the supplemental list.

A justice may, of course, resign and he may be removed at the discretion of the Lord Chancellor or, as the case may be, the Chancellor of the Duchy of Lancaster. There are no particular grounds on which a justice may be removed. The most usual ground is non-attendance. Justices who have held high judicial office or are chairmen or deputy-chairmen of quarter sessions go on the supplemental list when they become seventy-five. This is in line with the law that High Court judges have to retire at the age of seventy-five.

Those who wish to apply to become justices should write to the secretary of the Advisory Committee for their area or preferably get someone else, who is prepared to recommend them, to write to the Secretary.

Once anyone is appointed as a justice, he or she is eligible to sit either at petty sessions, that is, the ordinary magistrates' court, or at county quarter sessions. But far fewer justices now sit at quarter sessions and their number is limited to eight at any court. If the Beeching Commission's proposals are adopted they will only sit in an advisory capacity at quarter sessions except in juvenile appeals. Special training is given to those justices who are appointed to a juvenile court. This is in addition to the basic training.

Justices try certain matrimonial disputes, bastardy cases and have certain other civil jurisdiction, but their main work is the trial of criminal cases. Every criminal case, however important, starts before justices (unless it comes before a stipendiary magistrate, of whom there are under fifty). If it is a case which justices have no power to try, their only duties are to listen to the evidence, control the proceedings in the court and then decide whether there is a case for committal for trial at quarter sessions or assizes. They also deal with any question of bail. From their decision on bail there is an appeal to a High Court judge. The justices' clerk is either a solicitor or a barrister. When justices try a case their decision is by a majority.

Subject to certain exceptions, justices must reside in or within fifteen miles of the area to which they are appointed.

The main criticisms directed at the way in which justices carry out their duties today concern the variations between the sentences of one Bench and another and, to a lesser extent, alleged bias against motorists. This allegation of bias is

curious. Justices are really a sort of select and superior jury.
It is notorious that ordinary juries are absurdly lenient towards
motorists, to say the least of it, and, indeed, have been known
on a good many occasions to break their oaths by acquitting
motorists who are plainly guilty. In non-motoring cases juries
normally behave in a sensible and fair-minded way. The
reason for their not doing so in some motoring cases is simply
because they can visualise themselves charged with the same
offence. " There but for the grace of God go I."

There are certainly as many motorists among justices as
there are among juries but I doubt if bias is often shown by
a Bench in favour of a motorist. (Ask the Motoring Associa-
tions.) This at least shows the sense of responsibility which
justices feel once they are appointed, though no doubt a
defendant to a motoring charge would prefer a little less sense
of responsibility and a little more fellow-feeling.

Some Benches have tariffs for minor offences (such as
parking or the like) and it is understandable that the motorist
who is charged the ordinary fee, when he feels that his case is
out of the ordinary, should be aggrieved. Unquestionably the
matter of penalty may vary from Bench to Bench but, where
justices have to try a case of careless driving or a more serious
driving offence, I do not believe that they show any more bias
against the accused than a stipendiary magistrate or a judge
would show. It is quite understandable that a motorist, who
nearly always believes himself to be in the right, feels that
anyone who says he is in the wrong is biassed. I have already
dealt with the difficulty of trying accident cases. They can
seldom be tried to the satisfaction of everyone.

Apart from motoring cases the main criticisms of justices
are that they are too lenient or too severe. Sometimes leniency
in a vandalism case, for example, is contrasted with severity

in a case of stealing. It is right that the Press and others should criticise the findings of courts of law, but what has to be remembered is that these criticisms are mainly based on what appears in the newspapers, which in most cases have insufficient space to devote to one particular case. In consequence it often happens that those who criticise have not all the facts before them.

In exactly the same way the sentences of High Court judges can be compared and columnists will complain that one judge is too lenient and another too severe. They may be right but no one who did not hear both cases in full is really in a position to criticise. The vast majority of cases can only be reported in a condensed form and it is quite impossible for the most skilled reporter to ensure that every important factor, having a bearing on the sentence, is in his report as published. For example, the offence of stealing a one-pound note may be fairly trivial if committed on impulse, but serious if done in pursuance of a conspiracy. Yet each charge may simply appear as, " did steal a one-pound note."

As long as there are human beings there will be variations in sentence. No two minds think exactly alike. Justices are appointed because it is thought that they are people with a sense of responsibility who are likely to discharge their difficult duties with care and fairness. They are bound to differ in their views about a case. That indeed is why they have been appointed. So far as possible the Lord Chancellor seeks to get a balanced Bench, where the Tory landowner will sit next to the trade union official. There must of course be failures, and there must be some people who are unsuited to the position. But, by and large, I do not believe this happens except in the tiny minority of cases and it must be remembered that in a year the Benches try many hundred thousand cases.

The main object of the training which every newly appointed justice has to undergo is reduction in the diversity of sentences. I wonder whether standardisation of sentences is necessarily a good thing. It is impossible to obtain anything like perfection in the administration of justice. Who can say with certainty what is a right sentence? When justices come to consider what the proper sentence is in a particular case they should not have to be thinking to themselves: " Now, what were we told in Lecture 1 about this kind of case? " They should be considering all the facts of the case, they will have been told the maximum (and very occasionally the minimum) sentence which the law prescribes and they will have read in the newspapers the way in which cases of that kind are dealt with elsewhere. Subject, then, to the law's requirements I think that they should decide on the appropriate sentence solely by discussion among themselves, having regard to all the circumstances.

Of course, by the use of computers you *could* do away with the necessity for lawyers and judges. The suspected offender would be taken by a policeman to the C.C.C.—not the Central Criminal Court but the Computer Centre (Criminal). The policeman would feed into the computer all the facts which he knew and the computer would say what were the man's chances of being convicted. If they were, say, three-to-one against acquittal, the policeman would put on the table, face down, four cards, three with " Guilty " on them and one with " Not Guilty ". The suspect would choose one. If he was lucky, he would go free. If not, he would go on to the sentencing computer which would tell him what the penalty was. Similarly, in civil cases the parties would go to the Computer Centre (Civil) and feed the facts into a computer. They would then be told what the chances were of one side or the other winning, and they would draw for it. Much cheaper and quicker. But, unless this is what the public want, I suggest that attempts to computerise justice should be strongly resisted, except perhaps in really trivial cases, such as those which can be dealt with by on-the-spot fines payable to the court.

I expressed the view early in this lecture that judges are not fully qualified to pass sentence in serious cases and that, if they pass sentence at all, their sentences should be reviewed by a special panel. Although my reasons for this view could be said to apply to the less serious offences where a sentence of imprisonment may be awarded by justices, I do not think on balance that they do.

The maximum sentence of imprisonment which justices can pass is one year. It would take a considerable time, sometimes months, to get all the information which may be necessary for the panel to enable it to pass or review a sentence. In the serious cases tried by a judge the offender will be in prison while these inquiries are being made. The months he spends there will count against his sentence. But in the case of justices either the offender will be on bail or in prison while the additional inquiries are made. If he is on bail, it will be highly undesirable to keep the possible sentence hanging over his head for at least weeks and possibly months. Alternatively, if he is in prison and it is subsequently decided that he ought not to have been sent there, a serious injustice may have been done. It must also be remembered that, if justices do decide to send a person to prison, it is always possible for the Home Secretary to advise the Sovereign to mitigate the penalty.

I am now going to deal with the personal liability of a justice to pay the costs of an appeal against his decision. Some little time ago the High Court ordered a Bench of three magistrates to pay such costs. The Lord Chancellor on appeal to him varied the order by deciding that only the chairman should pay the costs. Is it right that any judge or justice should be liable to pay the costs of a successful appeal against his decision? If he has behaved with gross impropriety he can be removed from office either by the Sovereign on an address from both Houses of Parliament or, in the case of a lesser judge or a justice, by the Lord Chancellor. In such cases the costs ought obviously not to be borne by the parties, but should they be borne by the offending tribunal or by the Treasury or by the local authority?

A High Court judge cannot, in any circumstances, be ordered to pay costs but a county court judge or a stipendiary magistrate or a justice can be so ordered in certain cases. I do not know of any case this century in which such an order has been made against a professional judge or magistrate. Personally I do not consider that anyone sitting in a judicial capacity should have hanging over his head the faintest possibility that he may be financially worse off if he does a particular thing in discharge of his judicial duties.

Where there has been impropriety it is right that the judge or magistrate should be reproved by a higher court or, if the misbehaviour is serious enough, removed from office. It is also right that public funds, not the parties, should bear the costs. But should a judge or magistrate ever be put into the position of having to adapt his behaviour to suit his pocket?

In the case just mentioned the Lord Chancellor decided that the chairman was fit to remain on the Bench. It was reported in the Press that when the chairman complained to the Lord Chancellor's department of having to pay the costs, although he was still considered fit to sit on the Bench, a spokesman for the Lord Chancellor's department said that appeal court judges from time to time severely criticised the judges in the court below but that they were not removed from office. To which the chairman very reasonably replied: "They are not fined £200," the amount of the costs.

It may be said that it is very rare indeed that such an order is made against a justice and that it may be no bad thing to remind justices of the dangers of interrupting a case too much (which was the gist of the complaint against the chairman in question). But surely the power to remove is a far greater sanction than any other. And, if justices need reminding, why not High Court judges also?

Although my next comments do not only affect justices but relate to all courts it seems an appropriate place in which to refer generally to the costs of appeals. Theoretically the cost to an individual of obtaining justice should be nothing, but that could only occur in a perfect state. So litigation will always be expensive to individuals who indulge or are caught up in it. Unless he has free legal aid, a man must in this imperfect world expect to have to pay for going or being taken to law. But, having paid to get a judge's decision, should he have to pay more if that decision is wrong? Should there not be some system by which the cost of meritorious appeals should be borne by the state, if and when it can afford it? Mr. Vergottis is certainly entitled to think that our law is strange. In the proceedings between him and Mr. Onassis and Madame Callas five superior court judges decided in his favour (three judges in the Court of Appeal and two in the House of Lords) and only four against him. Yet he lost by a majority of three to two in the House of Lords. Should not the cost of such judicial disagreements be paid, not by one or more of the judges, or by the parties, but by the State?

All judges want to give a correct decision but even the greatest cannot always be right. One judge was so affected

in his conscience by the thought that he had done an injustice
to a particular litigant that he left him a legacy in his will by
way of amends. This was Sir Soulden Lawrence in the early
nineteenth century. But, if he thought by this to make his
passage to Heaven any easier, he ought not to have succeeded.
All that the judge did was to make his relatives or friends pay
for his mistake. If the judge during his lifetime had sent the
money anonymously to the litigant that would have been a
different matter (though it might have been unjudicial), but
to visit his own mistake on the heads of his children or other
relatives or his friends seems a pretty odd way of doing
justice.

I have two final and very important comments to make
about justices. The first is that the same tradition of integrity
on the Bench appears to exist among justices as it does among
professional judges. Occasionally a justice commits a serious
crime. Sometimes the crime is corruption in regard to local
affairs. Such a man is obviously below the standard required
for appointment to the magistracy. By mischance he has been
appointed. Yet it appears that never in his capacity of a
justice has he allowed his criminal tendencies to come to
the fore. There is certainly no case in the last hundred years
where a justice has been charged with accepting a bribe or
conspiring to defeat the ends of justice. The tradition of
integrity is too strong even for the occasional justice who,
unknown to those who appointed him, has criminal tendencies.

Secondly it should be appreciated that our present system
not only saves the country a very large sum of money but
would take many, many years to replace, if indeed it could ever
be replaced satisfactorily within a foreseeable period. At
present there are just under fifty stipendiary magistrates and
even now there are complaints that the Lord Chancellor has

difficulty in finding candidates for that position of a sufficiently high standard. If justices were to be replaced by professional magistrates, hundreds at least would be required. Such numbers could not be obtained without substantially lowering the standard. Is it better to have third- or fourth-rate lawyers deciding these cases or laymen (advised by a competent lawyer) who are now chosen from all ranks of society and who traditionally have discharged this office for hundreds of years with considerable success in the vast majority of cases? We are certainly unique among European nations in having a system whereby unpaid laymen try cases. The standard of justice would in my view be lowered if lay justices were replaced by inexperienced or incompetent professional magistrates and the cost in money would be very substantial indeed, even if the present salaries were not increased.

I should say something about the Court of Appeal (Criminal Division). This court is now part of the Court of Appeal and usually consists of the Lord Chief Justice and two Lords Justices. A number of High Court judges also sit from time to time. The court used to be called the Court of Criminal Appeal and normally consisted of the Lord Chief Justice and two High Court judges. The change was made mainly because it ˢ thought unsatisfactory that appeals from High Court should be heard by other High Court judges. It was ₜter that they should be heard by a higher court.

t of Criminal Appeal had for many years an ᵃtion. Its object was a good one, namely, ˢtice, but in many cases it set about it ᵒften gave the appearance of being ᵍls and not to listen to argument.

ᵣ. *of Police for City of London* t of Criminal Appeal listened to

the argument for the appellant for one hour and, without
calling upon counsel for the Crown, dismissed the appeal.
Fortunately for the appellant the Attorney-General certified
that an important point of law was involved and that it was in
the public interest that a further appeal should be brought.
The case was accordingly heard later by the House of Lords.
A very distinguished House heard the appeal. It consisted of
Lord Maugham (the Lord Chancellor), Lord Atkin, Lord
Macmillan, Lord Porter and Lord Wright. These five judges
heard the case for four days and unanimously allowed the
appeal. The argument in each court was put forward by the
same leading counsel (who is now a distinguished judge) and
the Court of Criminal Appeal had no excuse whatever for the
wrong-headed and arbitrary way in which they heard the
appeal.

That was the standard of that court at the time. It was a
long time before Lord Goddard became Lord Chief Justice,
but a tradition once established tends to remain far too long
even though the successors to that tradition do not themselves
approve of it. The Court of Criminal Appeal who heard
R. v. *Milne* (*supra*) consisted of the same judges who dealt
with the other case to which I referred earlier when a judge at
the Old Bailey had promised a prisoner that he would not send
him to prison if he pleaded Guilty (pages 71–75).

But in criticising the Court of Criminal Appeal one shoul
have some sympathy with the members of that court. The v
majority of appellants were guilty and deserved their senter
and most of the appeals were frivolous. The judges h
read an immense number of documents taking many ho
in nine cases out of ten or probably in a much higher
tion of cases there was nothing to be said for the app
must have been difficult for some judges not

consciously or unconsciously, a prejudice against appeals after years of such experience.

One should have even more sympathy for the present Court of Appeal (Criminal Division) as appeals are vastly more in number than they were and there is certainly no higher percentage of meritorious appeals. Indeed, probably, the percentage is much lower. Perhaps it is wrong that judges should sit on this court for too long, lest in the end they develop a prejudice which is alien to their judicial nature, but such a suggestion could not at present be adopted as there are insufficient numbers of Lords Justices available.

I have dealt with the main heads of complaints against judges but there are others which may not come exactly under any one of those heads. It is said, for example, that some judges think the court's time more important than that of the litigants and refuse adjournments unnecessarily. There have indeed been some judges in whose court it would be absolutely fatal to say that the reason for an application for an adjournment was because the parties were not ready. Such applications had to be, as the late Mr. Justice Swift would say, " wrapped-up." It is said that on one occasion a young barrister made an application to him for an adjournment and started to say that his client was not ready. Mr. Justice Swift told him to " wrap it up " and when the young man did not understand what was being said to him, the judge told him to wait and hear the next application. This application was made by a very experienced advocate who gave every conceivable ground for adjourning the case—the illness of his client, the absence of the chief witness abroad, one fire having destroyed the factory where the accident took place and another fire having destroyed all the documents in the solicitor's office and so on. When that counsel had finished and his case had been duly adjourned, Mr. Justice Swift turned to the young man and said: " Now, Mr. Jones, you know what I mean by ' wrapping it up '."

Unfortunately this was all too true in the days when I was at the Bar and may be true still.   Obviously cases ought to be ready for trial on the day which is appointed for their hearing, unless there is a very good reason.   But, even when the failure to be ready is due to carelessness or laxity of some kind, an adjournment should be granted if a fair trial of the action is not likely to be reached without it.   If, in the result, the judge has nothing to do that day he should go and play golf.   It is very important that the parties concerned should think they are going to have a fair trial.   If an adjournment is refused when their solicitor tells them that they are not ready for the trial, they may well believe (and it may be the fact) that, if they lose the case, it is owing to the trial not having been adjourned.

When you are seeking to attain justice, I should have thought that the fact that the parties were not ready to put their case properly was the best possible ground for asking for an adjournment and, if it is still the worst, it is not so much a reflection upon the solicitors who fail to prepare for trial as upon the judges who in those circumstances refuse to grant an adjournment.   If there are no excusable grounds for not being ready, orders to pay costs and strictures from the Bench (which would be reported in the Press) should be quite sufficient to deter people from making a regular practice of not being ready and thus getting the lists into disorder.

The value of a judge's time, says one critic, while high, is often overrated and often has the consequence that scores of other professional people and witnesses with useful jobs have to be kept in attendance and waiting to suit the judge's convenience. " There is no reason why the judge should not when possible wait to suit the convenience of a large number of other people."

I think more could be done to suit the convenience of witnesses and parties, but it is often impossible to prevent them from being kept idle for a long time. The order of witnesses in a case may suddenly change, or it may be necessary to recall a witness. So many things may happen in the course of a case that, unless all or nearly all of the witnesses are present or available at short notice all the time, the result may be that a case takes very much longer to try and may have to be adjourned several times, to the far greater inconvenience of most people concerned in it. The Beeching Commission has made suggestions for improving the situation.

I agree that there have been judges in the past and there are probably some still who value their own time and their dignity too highly. Perhaps one of my few virtues as a judge was that I never minded waiting for counsel who were trying to settle a case, even if it meant that I had nothing whatever to do except read the paper. If a long case was settled on the day for which it was fixed and nothing else had been put in the list, I did not complain at the shocking waste of judicial time but happily went home to do other things.

Complaints are made of the time which some judges take to try a case. This is partly caused by the judge writing out his version of the evidence in longhand. As far as I can see, the necessity for a judge to write out the evidence in longhand will probably remain until every court has a machine which will produce the evidence at dictation speed in front of the judge as he sits there. A judge must at all times be able to refer back to the evidence and unless he has his own note of it, at present he has to wait for a transcript of the shorthand note or for the particular shorthand writer to read back his notes from his shorthand notebook. But shorthand writers change over during the day and, therefore, if a judge does not take a note, he might be unable to find out what was said until the next day. This might necessitate an adjournment. Tape-recorders do not help very much because of the time that it would sometimes take to find out the exact place on the tape-recorder where the passage occurred. There are a few judges who take down notes in shorthand, and some judges can write longhand very quickly. But others can only write slowly, and undoubtedly this does delay a trial.

Until the machine to which I have referred is provided for all judges, the only solution would be to require every judge to learn shorthand before his appointment. I should have hated it, but it may be that in the interests of quicker justice this requirement should be made. If it were, to a certain extent this would be a help to the Bar because what would happen would probably be that all barristers would learn shorthand, so that, by the time the question of their elevation to the Bench arose, they would have the necessary shorthand qualification and this would be a help to them in their practice.

It is occasionally complained that judges alter their judgments after they have delivered them. As I pointed out earlier, most judgments are delivered *ex tempore* and the complaint is that, if the case is reported in one of the law reports, it is sometimes in a slightly different form from that in which it was delivered. This is true, but there is a good reason for it. In the first place no judge would ever dream of altering any of the essentials of his judgment. Any alterations that he makes do not affect the parties at all. What a judge is entitled to do is this. In the first place he may correct any bad grammar— get rid of any split infinitives if he does not like them—and improve the English if it seems to require it. The more important thing which he does, if he makes any other alteration, is for the benefit of the law as a whole. During the course of his judgment in dealing with a point of law he may have gone further than was necessary for the purposes of the case and either put something in too wide terms or said something which was unnecessary for the purpose of deciding the particular matter which he was trying. Such a statement is called by lawyers an *obiter dictum*. It is not binding on other judges but they will always pay attention to it, particularly if the judge is known to be a great lawyer, *e.g.* Lord Atkin. If, on consideration, the judge thinks that his statement of the law was too wide or that his *obiter dictum* was doubtful, or even wrong, he may delete it from the judgment or modify it. And the altered version will appear in the law report. The parties will have a copy of the original judgment just the same, and, if they want to argue that because he made a mistake of that kind, he may have made a mistake which went to the root of the case, they can do so. Nothing is concealed from anyone except to some extent from posterity, and, as I have said, this is an advantage. If the alteration were not made and the *obiter dictum* appeared in the law reports it might be relied upon in a later case, which might be decided wrongly in consequence.

I should make it plain that the judge is not altering the judgment itself, only his reasons for giving that judgment. The judgment once recorded cannot be altered except for obvious clerical errors or similar mistakes. Once a Chief Justice (Ralph de Hengham) out of compassion reduced a man's fine after it had been entered on the record. The fine had been a mark (about 13s. 4d.) but it was too much for the man and the Chief Justice halved it. For this act of charity he was himself fined 8,000 marks. This was in the thirteenth century and since then no judge has altered the record again in a hurry, although the story is in fact of doubtful authenticity.

The editor of one newspaper had the impression that in recent years judges appear to have become tools of the Establishment and much less robust in defending the freedom of the ordinary citizen.

I was surprised at this criticism if it was intended to mean that the judges ran with the government of the day, because they certainly do not. Still less do they run with the civil servants of the day. I can only think of one case where it was at first suggested that judges had been influenced by the wishes of the Establishment. On examination this criticism turned out to be wholly without foundation. I dealt with this case in full in my book *Tipping the Scales* (pp. 181–189).

The statement by another editor requires consideration. He writes:

" Lawyers are notoriously slipshod with their homework but under the present system a plaintiff must sit quietly and listen to mistakes being pronounced in court. This is often due to the incompetence of counsel, bad briefing by solicitors and elderly judges frequently misunderstanding the whole case."

This editor has obviously had an unfortunate experience of lawyers and courts, but he certainly has a point about the litigants, the parties most concerned in a case, not being able to intervene. It must sometimes be very frustrating for Mr. Jones, when he hears Mrs. Brown saying something which is completely untrue and which he can prove to be untrue, if he is not allowed to say so there and then. But obviously cases could not be conducted satisfactorily if everybody could keep on interrupting as and when he pleased.

It is always open to a judge, who sees someone in court

obviously affected by something that has been said, to stop the proceedings for a moment and to say something like this: " Mr. Jones, if you don't agree with what is being said, you will have an opportunity of giving your version later. In the meantime, if you would like to go and speak to your solicitor or counsel and tell him something privately, I will stop the case for a moment to give you that opportunity." This behaviour on the part of a judge will do a good deal to make it easier for people, who are wholly unused to court procedure, to conduct themselves with propriety in court without feeling too frustrated. It will also give them the feeling that their case is being fairly and fully heard. What happens too often is that the usher, and very likely the man's own solicitor and counsel too, tell him to shut up. And that is not a way in which to make him feel that justice has been done if in the end he happens to lose the case.

The method of stopping a case and giving a person an opportunity to speak to his advocate is perhaps not used often enough. It is even more important in criminal cases where the man in the dock (even though guilty) may feel horribly frustrated if not helped in this way from time to time.

Another editor complains " of a system by which it is impossible for a defence lawyer to intervene or interrupt the judge's views which are often demonstrably inaccurate." If this editor means that you must not interrupt a judge's judgment or summing-up, even that is wrong because you can at least try to point out an inaccuracy, especially in a summing-up. It is true that a judge can refuse to allow you to interrupt but the majority of judges today would allow such an interruption if it appeared to be a sensible one. If the editor is not referring to a judgment or summing-up, he is completely wrong. Counsel may always intervene during a case to point out an inaccuracy either on the part of his opponent or on the part of the judge.

The same editor asks why judges don't call in experts to assist them, *e.g.* a child psychologist. There is power in the judge, with the consent of the parties, to appoint an assessor to assist him in the trying of an action where any technical questions are involved. This power could be exercised in a medical, engineering, building or any technical case. In the Admiralty Division the judge is assisted by nautical assessors. I think it might be of considerable advantage if this power were used more frequently. The employment of an assessor increases the cost to the parties but in most cases the extra expense will be offset by the shorter time in which the case can be tried. This was certainly my experience.

Nearly everything which I have so far said applies equally to county court judges and stipendiary magistrates but I now want to deal with matters which only concern those lesser judges.

A law student writes that it seems to be inherent in the way that county court judges and stipendiary magistrates are appointed that a fair number of them should be disappointing because they are disappointed, and he adds that it is notorious that some very unsatisfactory stipendiary magistrates were unsuccessful silks. He says that promotion from county court to High Court is so rare that most county court judges are men who have given up hope of the High Court Bench or a more lucrative career at the Bar and he suggests that a more reliable judiciary for the future requires the creation of a judicial ladder. Another somewhat more cynical statement about magistrates was that " in London you are tried by an unsuccessful barrister and in the country you are tried by three successful tradesmen."

I will deal with county court judges first. Out of my random sample of forty-five county court judges, one in five had taken silk before appointment. It is perfectly true that the position of county court judges is not high in the legal hierarchy. It is also true that in the past some barristers who became county court judges were not doing particularly well at the Bar at the time when they accepted the appointment to the Bench. One of them became one of the best county court judges of this century. His practice at the Bar was negligible. His reputation as a judge became very high indeed. His name was Judge Snagge and many lawyers thought that he should have been promoted to the High Court. On the other hand, some judges suffer a reduction in income when they accept the appointment.

One of the advantages of a judicial appointment is the fact that it carries with it a pension and a widow's pension. At the present rate of income tax and surtax a barrister who has saved no substantial capital but is earning a large income at the Bar, would be better off financially as a county court judge. The approximate net difference between the £11,500 a year of the High Court judge and the current salary of a county court judge of £6,550 is between about £1,000 and £2,000 depending on the other income, if any, of the judges concerned. A married county court judge receives a pension after fifteen years' service (provided he is 65 at the time of retirement) of half his salary. It would require a very substantial capital sum to produce such an income.

A county court judge has very much more spare time than a High Court judge during the term and practically no homework. He doesn't have to travel unless he has accepted a circuit where there is a lot of travelling and even then he lives at home. London judges normally have one court only, and go backwards and forwards to that court. Although the sounding of the trumpet at assizes may be some small consolation to a few judges, most judges would prefer the happiness which comes from living with their wives and families. One of the reasons for the unexpected resignation earlier this year of an eminent 52-year-old High Court judge, after only two years' service, may well have been that he found the long periods of absence from his family unacceptable.

Then, there is always the possibility that a Queen's Bench judge will be called upon to serve in the Court of Appeal (Criminal Division). When a judge is to sit in that court on a Monday he will have little time during the previous weekend for anything except reading the papers with which he is concerned. This will involve reading the full shorthand note of trials which have taken hours, days or even weeks.

It is certainly no sinecure to be a High Court judge today. And though the knighthood which it carries is pleasant for the judge and his wife for a month or two, they soon get used to it, and for many people that and the larger salary will not make up for the prolonged periods of separation and the much harder work. A county court judge is never burdened with criminal appeals. Moreover, in the main, his work is much easier and involves infinitely fewer difficult points of law. In consequence, whereas a High Court judge may have to reserve judgment on quite a number of occasions, most county court judges rarely have to reserve judgment. When a judge does reserve his judgment it means that he has to write it out at home and do such research as he may consider necessary in order to enable him to arrive at a decision. I have known a county court judge who never reserved a single judgment in the whole of his career. I tried many thousands of cases, and only reserved judgment on three occasions.

There is no doubt in my mind that the High Court judge more than earns the difference between his salary and that of a county court judge.

The standard of a county court judge today is certainly higher than it was when I came to the Bar in 1923 and for some time afterwards. Unquestionably one good result of taxation is that barristers with substantial practices apply for county court judgeships as the happy climax to a successful career. Few, if any, county court judges take the appointment in the hope or the expectation of being promoted to the High Court. It is true that there are more promotions than there used to be but they are few and the law student is right in thinking that the possibility of promotion is not normally an inducement to a barrister to become a county court judge. I may be biassed but I think that the present standard of these judges is fully high enough to deal with the work which they have to undertake. I am far more concerned about the standard of the forty new judges proposed in the Beeching Report, even though they are only appointed gradually. If forty new judges are to be appointed without trial, it may well be that there will be a lowering of standards. The Government might be better advised to abolish road accident cases and maintain the present standard of the judiciary.

I have a comment to make about county court judges, although I realise that some judges and others may think that the comment is wholly without foundation, and I recognise that it may be. County court judges often deal with litigants in person and, in particular, they deal with debtors and people against whom a possession order is sought. One point of view is that the judge is simply there to try cases, and, however sympathetic and compassionate he may be, once he has given his decision, that is an end of the matter. If a person needs help or advice of any kind after a decision has been given he should apply to the Citizens' Advice Bureau or his Member of Parliament or to the local Children's Officer or to some other welfare institution or individual.

There is no problem in the magistrates' courts. They have a probation officer, and a magistrate frequently asks him to interview either a defendant or a witness who appears to need help or advice. There is no such help officially available in the county court. My own view is that there should be. A sort of unofficial welfare service was started in my court. This, of course, could only be done with the assistance of public-spirited people anxious to help. Through the good offices of the Institute of Directors such people were found. In particular one exceptionally enthusiastic and unselfish retired director has done a tremendous amount of good not only in the Willesden area but also by arranging for the scheme to be adopted in other courts. The cases in which assistance has been given range from a case where a man was saved from losing a property worth £3,000 entirely through his own stupidity to cases where all that could be done was to comfort a person and show him that every man's hand was not against him.

Many of the people who come before a county court are unable to cope with the problems of life, they need help and they do not know how to ask for it. I think that if a judge sees someone who needs help, he should try to arrange for him to have it, provided this can be done without affecting the other party to the litigation. Sometimes this unofficial welfare officer is able to help both sides. More often it is only one party who requires it and, when this help is given, it must be given without affecting the other party in the least degree.

I think this ought to be done in every county court. A number of others have adopted it, but I feel sure that there are judges who consider it unnecessary or wrong. Those who think it unnecessary must suffer severely from lack of imagination but I fully see the argument of those who think it wrong. It certainly would be wrong if the judge himself became involved. Equally it would be wrong if the other party to the litigation felt that his opponent, because he was poor or unhappy, had the ear of the judge or was being helped unfairly. But, provided the judge merely sets the wheels of welfare in motion without in any way affecting the other people concerned in the case, it appears to me that it is not merely right that this should be done but that the absence of a welfare system of this kind in the county court is a serious omission.

The county court is in some ways the equivalent, on the civil side, of the magistrates' court and if the latter needs a welfare officer (and it certainly does), so does the former. In the High Court nearly every litigant has solicitors and counsel to help and advise him. In spite of legal aid there are many litigants in the county court—and they are always the least able to look after themselves—who have no such help. Inadequate people who need help and come in front of a county court judge should be channelled in some direction where help will be given to them.

Incidentally, the county courts in London and some other places appear to be the only courts, as far as I know, where there is no delay. In these courts a litigant enters his action on a particular day and it will be tried within six or seven weeks of that day. Often the action is too complicated for such an early trial and the solicitors on each side want and obtain a later date. Cases are always heard upon the day for which they are fixed and are never adjourned for want of time.

This happy state of affairs is due to the fact that the system operating in London for the trial of cases in the county court is about as good as a judicial system can be. If a judge comes to court on a particular day and it looks as though the list contains too many cases for him to try on that day, his clerk can telephone to the Lord Chancellor's department and ask for another judge to be sent to assist with the list. The other judge is sometimes a " floating " judge [2] but more often, if the notice is very short, he will be a deputy judge and that is the only objection to the system. There might be difficult cases which the parties did not want to be tried by anyone under the rank of a full judge. But even this difficulty can sometimes be avoided by appointing as deputy judge a retired judge who is still quite young enough to try cases properly.

All that is required for a successful judicial system is enough satisfactory judges and enough courts.

It is because this simple expedient has not been applied to the High Court and to magistrates' courts that there have been the appalling delays of which complaint has justifiably been made.

This brings me to the stipendiary magistrates. The situation of the magistrates' courts in London is a scandal. The magistrate has far too many cases in his list and there are long, unavoidable delays. Even when an accused person is on bail it is highly undesirable that he should have a charge hanging over him for long. When he is in prison it may be a gross injustice. Motorists' offences are tried often many months after they are alleged to have taken place. I have already referred to the difficulty of trying accident cases. To a lesser extent the magistrate has the same difficulty. I say " to a lesser extent," however, because in his case he has to be satisfied of the defendant's guilt beyond all reasonable

---

[2] A judge who has no court of his own and goes to any court where he may be required.

doubt. It is easier to have a doubt than to decide on the probabilities.

The pressure on the magistrates is so great that it is not surprising that, when young and inefficient or old and prolix advocates appear in front of them, some of them show irritation. The speed at which magistrates have to work is absurd and some defendants may well think it better to plead Guilty than to annoy an overworked magistrate. This is the fault of successive governments since the war. Obviously the building of houses and rebuilding of hospitals was a first priority, but the building of offices was not. It would have been perfectly possible for governments in the years after the war to have ensured that there were sufficient magistrates' courts in London and then to have appointed sufficient magistrates to deal with the volume of work.

It may be that special courts will be created to try motoring cases or at any rate the less serious ones, and, if this happens, it will of course relieve magistrates of a great deal of work. But before it can happen the same problem will arise. Where are they to sit? Because of the lack of foresight of successive governments it will be extremely difficult to find suitable premises to be adapted for courts.

But, even when this happens, even when magistrates no longer have to work at breakneck speed, they will have inherited an unfortunate legacy that it will be very difficult for them to cast aside. It is unlikely that some of those who are at present sitting as magistrates will ever be able to suffer fools with that gladness which is necessary in small courts. It is so important that everyone should feel his case has been fairly and carefully heard and that he has not lost it, for example, because his advocate talked too much. I gather that most stipendiaries in London are amazingly patient, but it is not surprising that there are exceptions.

I am not saying that there are not times when a High Court or county court judge may not feel impatient, nor am I saying that he never shows signs of this impatience. When a certain barrister, Mr. Crabtree (that was not his real name but he was a very real person), appeared before me—Mr. Crabtree whose sentences had no beginning, middle or end and whose idea of cross-examining a witness was to ask three or four irrelevant questions, few of them complete and all of them before the witness had time to try to answer even the first fragment of a question—when he appeared in front of me, I repressed a sigh, but the one thing I could be sure of was that I was in no hurry. The result of the system to which I have referred was that there was never a sense of urgency or speed when cases were being tried.

Whether or not a motorist is convicted of careless driving is a very important matter from his point of view. Nearly all motorists who plead Not Guilty think they are in the right and, whatever the decision, they will continue to think so. But at least they should have the feeling that their case has been fairly heard in full without any signs of impatience from the magistrate. And there should be time for more than: " I find the case proved and there will be a fine of £5." Why did the magistrate ignore the independent witness? Did he disbelieve me when I said that I was only going at 25 miles per hour? Did he believe Mr. X who had told the police something different from what he said in the witness-box? And so on and so on.

These are questions which a defeated litigant, particularly a convicted motorist, wants answered and he is entitled to have an answer. In the county court he would normally hear the judge's reasons in full, however small the case. Today the unfortunate magistrate has no time to do this and cannot at all be blamed for getting on with the next case. If he did not, someone would stay in prison even longer than he does at present. But, if ever there are sufficient courts and sufficient magistrates to enable cases to be taken at a proper pace, magistrates should give reasons for their decisions.

The comments which I have made about the standard of barrister likely to be attracted to the county court Bench apply to a certain extent also to magistrates. The salary of a magistrate is not much below that of a county court judge but there are other distinctions. His position is lower in the judicial hierarchy and he does not have the pleasure of being called Judge by acquaintances and strangers. There has been no example of a magistrate being promoted to the High Court or county court Bench since I came to the Bar in 1923, but he does very occasionally become a full-time chairman of quarter sessions.

To qualify for pension as a stipendiary he has to do twenty years as opposed to the county court judge's fifteen. There seems to be no logical reason for this. A magistrate has to work quite as hard as a judge.

The criminal Bar today is doing so well as a result of the prevalence of crime and the amount of legal aid which is given to alleged criminals that it may become more difficult to obtain suitable stipendiary magistrates. I think it could be said today that if a barrister is not doing well at the criminal Bar, he certainly cannot be a good advocate. But even the large incomes which can now be made at the criminal Bar are subject to income tax and surtax and, unless a barrister has private means, the appointment to a magistracy, carrying with it as it does a reasonable salary and pension, has distinct advantages.

It would be difficult to recruit a higher standard of magistrate merely by increasing the salary, as there are many barristers who would not care to spend the rest of their working
lives dealing mainly with criminal cases. There are, no doubt,
one or two magistrates, as there are judges, who ought never to
have been appointed, and who would probably not have been
appointed if they had been tried out first. Apart from these,
the standard of magistrate appears to be high and again the
complaints arise because of the behaviour of the few.

A good many of the criticisms of magistrates have come
from people who have reason for not liking them, particularly
because they, or some relative or friend of theirs, have been
convicted in a magistrates' court. Here is a student's opinion:

" The magistrate appeared to me to feel substantial
middle-class glee at having these subversive nuisances
under his thumb and in finding specious reasons for
refusing time to pay, but of course it may well have been
the result of bias on my part."

Then a young man writes:

" He is disliked by many people including me, I mean
mainly because one of them gave my father a year's
suspension of driving which has practically destroyed his
business because he is in the motor trade."

A journalist writes:

" Many stipendiary magistrates have made a bad impression on people who sit in their courts every day. At least
one in London was notorious for intolerance, bad temper
and over-severe sentences. Many of the routine cases are
dealt with so quickly that the court and public are hardly
aware of what is happening."

The one magistrate might not have been appointed if he
had been given a trial run and, if there is in fact only one who is

as bad as that, then it is a great tribute to the self-control of the London magistrates.

A commentator who has had experience of local courts has an enormous respect for the stipendiaries in Thames, Woolwich and Greenwich where he has seen humour, humanity and humility. And a solicitor who has dealt with a large number of motoring cases says that the average motorist is impressed by the general meticulous approach of stipendiaries on questions of law and finds them dealing quite roughly with the police officer who presents his case badly. He also believes that the stipendiaries are impartial and unbiased and do not waste time and that these days they are unlikely to be eccentric. Of the typical stipendiary this solicitor continues:

" He is younger and is probably a motorist and understands their problems. A motorist regards every judge as being prosecution-minded but he is often agreeably surprised by the result and in the long run would probably hold very favourable views about the modern judge."

The last word about stipendiaries shall be with a police officer, who says that they are quick and efficient.

I have now dealt to the best of my ability with the judges in this country from the House of Lords down to the justices of the peace.

The House of Lords comes out of this survey completely unscathed. Indeed the only possible ground for complaint is the method of deciding appeals, which can have such odd results as in the case of Mr. Vergottis. But such cases are fortunately extremely rare and it is difficult to think of a satisfactory alternative. In any event it is no fault of their Lordships. The complaints made against the other judges mainly arise from the behaviour of a very few or because judges are human and make mistakes, like doctors. At least you live to complain after the mistake of a judge.

In her speech on the opening of the Queen's Building in the Law Courts in 1968 Her Majesty said:

> " As the independent custodians of the law, the judges bear a direct and personal burden of responsibility which makes their office a lonely and difficult one. We are fortunate that our judges are worthy inheritors of the great traditions of their predecessors."

I hope that what I have said in these lectures has shown that I am not blinded to judicial imperfections, indeed that my own enabled me the better to realise the imperfections of others. But in spite of these imperfections, and in spite of the fact that very occasionally a judge falls below the standard required of him publicly or privately, though never as far as professional integrity is concerned, I am convinced—if I may say so without disrespect—that Her Majesty's statement, as a general statement about judges as a whole, stands up to the most careful scrutiny, unlike George Orwell's " evil old man " with which I started these lectures.

INDEX

171

PRINTED IN GREAT BRITAIN
BY
THE EASTERN PRESS LTD.
OF LONDON AND READING